PENGUIN BOOKS

PICTURE ME GONE

Praise for *How I ___*

'A crunchily perfect knock-o___ ___ novel' – *Guardian*

'This is a powerful novel: time___ ___d luminous' – *Observer*

'That rare, rare thing, a first novel with a sustained, magical and utterly faultless voice' – Mark Haddon, author of *The Curious Incident of the Dog in the Night-Time*

'Intense and startling . . . heartbreakingly romantic' – *The Times*

'A wonderfully original voice' – *Mail on Sunday*

'Readers won't just read this book, they will let it possess them' – *Sunday Telegraph*

'It already feels like a classic, in the sense that you can't imagine a world without it' – *New Statesman*

Praise for *Just in Case*

'A modern *Catcher in the Rye* . . . written with generosity and warmth but also with an edgy, unpredictable intelligence' – *The Times*

'Unusual and engrossing' – *Independent*

'Intelligent, ironic and darkly funny' – *Time Out*

'Extraordinary' – *Observer*

'No one writes the way Meg Rosoff does – as if she's thrown away the rules. I love her fizzy honesty, her pluck, her way of untangling emotion through words' – Julie Myerson

Praise for *What I Was*

'Rosoff's most perfect novel . . . it's already a classic' – *Sunday Times*

'Thrilling and sensitively told' – *Observer*

'This exquisitely written novel, complete with amazing twist, is the teenage book of the year' – *Irish Times*

'A wonderfully warm, witty, intelligent and romantic story with a terrific whiplash in the tail. Textured, nuanced, dramatic and atmospheric, *What I Was* feels like a future classic' – *Daily Telegraph*

'Gently haunting' – *Metro*

'Compelling and all-encompassing . . . sucks the reader whole into its universe' – *Time Out*

'One of the best plot twists in a novel to be found this year' – *The Herald*

'A beautifully crafted tale that seems, like its protagonist, both enduringly old and fluently new' – *Los Angeles Times*

Praise for *The Bride's Farewell*

'Exhilarating . . . every sentence is crafted and weighted with beauty' – Amanda Craig, *Times on Saturday*

'An engaging, impeccably written novel' – *Independent on Sunday*

'A poetically charged romance, full of thorny emotional dilemmas . . . compelling' – *Marie Claire*

'Rosoff's writing is luminously beautiful' – *Financial Times*

'A wildly inventive romantic adventure' – *Red*

'It's not often that one comes across a book as richly detailed and layered as this . . . perfect' – *Daily Telegraph*

'A highly polished gem' – *The Scotsman*

'This exquisitely written journey into freedom, love and womanhood makes literature out of the pony tale' – *The Times*

Praise for *There Is No Dog*

'Rosoff's supple and subtle writing is at its finest . . . One must simply revel in the joyful singularity of Rosoff's latest masterpiece'
– Anthony McGowan, *Guardian*

'This confirms, yet again, that Rosoff can access that self-absorbed adolescent sensibility with remarkable accuracy and affection. Press this book into the hands of every feckless teenage boy you know'
– *Daily Mail*

'The excellent Rosoff returns with a bracingly audacious idea: what if God were a 19-year-old boy? It might explain a few things . . .'
– *Time Out*

'A wild, wise, cartwheeling explanation of life, the universe and everything. Given the glorious, eccentric, spectacular cock-up that is Planet Earth, the Creator can only have been a slack, male adolescent with a short attention span and an unruly sexual organ. I don't know why no one has worked this out before. It makes a whole lot more sense than particle physics. And, unlike Big Bang Theory, it's funny' – Mal Peet

PICTURE ME GONE

→ ME ←

GONE

Meg Rosoff

PENGUIN BOOKS

PENGUIN BOOKS

Published by the Penguin Group
Penguin Books Ltd, 80 Strand, London WC2R ORL, England
Penguin Group (USA) Inc., 375 Hudson Street, New York, New York 10014, USA
Penguin Group (Canada), 90 Eglinton Avenue East, Suite 700, Toronto, Ontario, Canada M4P 2Y3
(a division of Pearson Penguin Canada Inc.)
Penguin Ireland, 25 St Stephen's Green, Dublin 2, Ireland (a division of Penguin Books Ltd)
Penguin Group (Australia), 707 Collins Street, Melbourne, Victoria 3008, Australia
(a division of Pearson Australia Group Pty Ltd)
Penguin Books India Pvt Ltd, 11 Community Centre, Panchsheel Park, New Delhi – 110 017, India
Penguin Group (NZ), 67 Apollo Drive, Rosedale, Auckland 0632, New Zealand
(a division of Pearson New Zealand Ltd)
Penguin Books (South Africa) (Pty) Ltd, Block D, Rosebank Office Park, 181 Jan Smuts Avenue,
Parktown North, Gauteng 2193, South Africa
Penguin Books Ltd, Registered Offices: 80 Strand, London WC2R ORL, England

penguinbooks.com

Published by Penguin Books 2013
001

Text copyright © Meg Rosoff, 2013
All rights reserved

The moral right of the author has been asserted

Set in 11.9/16pt Sabon by Palimpsest Book Production Limited, Falkirk, Stirlingshire
Printed in Great Britain by Clays Ltd, St Ives plc

British Library Cataloguing in Publication Data
A CIP catalogue record for this book is available from the British Library

HARDBACK
ISBN: 978–0–141–34403–4

TRADE PAPERBACK
ISBN: 978–0–141–34404–1

www.greenpenguin.co.uk

MIX
Paper from
responsible sources
FSC
www.fsc.org   FSC™ C018179

Penguin Books is committed to a sustainable
future for our business, our readers and our planet.
This book is made from Forest Stewardship
Council™ certified paper.

For Brenda

1

The first Mila was a dog. A Bedlington terrier. It helps if you know these things. I'm not at all resentful at being named after a dog. In fact, I can imagine the scene exactly. *Mila*, my father would have said, that's a nice name. Forgetting where he'd heard it. And then my mother would remember the dog and ask if he was absolutely sure, and when he didn't answer, she would say, OK, then. Mila. And then looking at me think, Mila, my Mila.

I don't believe in reincarnation. It seems unlikely that I've inherited the soul of my grandfather's long-dead dog. But certain traits make me wonder. Was it entirely coincidence that Mila entered my father's head on the morning of my birth? Observing his daughter, one minute old, he thought first of the dog, Mila? Why?

My father and I are preparing for a journey to New York, to visit his oldest friend. But yesterday things changed. His friend's wife phoned to say he'd left home.

Left home? Gil asks. What on earth do you mean?

Disappeared, she says. No note. Nothing.

Gil looks confused. Nothing?

You'll still come? says the wife.

And when Gil is silent for a moment, thinking it through, she says, Please.

Yes, of course, Gil says, and slowly replaces the phone in its cradle.

He'll be back, Gil tells Marieka. He's just gone off by himself to think for a while. You know what he's like.

But why now? My mother is puzzled. When he knew you were coming? The timing is . . . peculiar.

Gil shrugs. By this time tomorrow he'll be back. I'm certain he will.

Marieka makes a doubtful noise but from where I'm crouched I can't see her face. What about Mila? she says.

A few things I know: It is Easter holiday and I am out of school. My mother is working all week in Holland and I cannot stay at home alone. My father lives inside his head and it is better for him to have company when he travels, to keep him on track. The tickets were bought two months ago.

We will both still go.

I enjoy my father's company and we make a good pair. Like my namesake, Mila the dog, I have a keen awareness of where I am and what I'm doing at all times. I am not given to dreaminess, have something of a terrier's determination. If there is something to notice, I will notice it first.

I am good at solving puzzles.

My packing is nearly finished when Marieka comes to say that she and Gil have decided I should still go. I am already arranging clues in my head, thinking through the possibilities, looking for a theory.

I have met my father's friend sometime in the distant past but I don't remember him. He is a legend in our family for once saving Gil's life. Without Matthew there would be no me. For this, I would like to thank him, though I never really get the chance.

It seems so long ago that we left London. Back then I was a child.

I am still, technically speaking, a child.

2

I know very little about Mila the dog. She belonged to my grandfather when he was a boy growing up in Lancashire and dogs like Mila were kept for ratting not pets. I found a dusty old photo of her in an album my father kept from childhood. Mostly it contains pictures of people I don't know. In the photo, the dog has a crouchy stance, as if she'd rather be running flat out. The person on the other side of the camera interests me greatly. Perhaps it is my grandfather, a boy who took enough pride in his ratting dog to keep a photo of her. Lots of people take pictures of their dogs now, but did they then? The dog is looking straight ahead. If it were his dog, wouldn't it turn to look?

This picture fills me with a deep sense of longing. *Saudade*, Gil would say. Portuguese. The longing for something loved and lost, something gone or unattainable.

I cannot explain the feeling of sadness I have looking at this picture. Mila the dog has been dead for eighty years.

Everyone calls my father Gil. Gil's childhood friend has walked out of the house he shared with his wife and baby. No one knows where he went or why. Matthew's wife phoned Gil, in case he wanted to change our plans. In case he'd heard something.

He hadn't. Not then.

We will take the train to the airport and it is important to remember our passports. Marieka tells me to take good care of myself and kisses me. She smiles and asks if I will be OK and I nod, because I will. She looks in Gil's direction and says, Take care of your father. She knows I will take care of him as best I can. Age is not always the best judge of competence.

The train doors close and we wave goodbye. I settle down against my father and breathe the smell of his jacket. He smells of books, ink, old coffee pushed to the back of the desk and wool, plus a hint of the cologne Marieka used to buy him; one he hasn't worn in years. The smell of his skin is too familiar to describe. It surprised me to discover that not everyone can identify people by their smell. Marieka says this makes me half dog at least.

I've seen the way dogs sniff people and other dogs on the street or when they return from another place. They want to put a picture together based on clues: Where have you been? Were there cats there? Did you eat meat? So. A wood fire. Mud. Lemons.

If I were a dog and smelled books, coffee and ink in a slightly tweedy wool jacket, I don't know whether I'd think, *That man translates books.* But that is what he does.

I've always wondered why humans developed so many languages. It complicates things. *Makes things interesting,* says Gil.

Today, we are going to America, where we won't need any extra languages. Gil ruffles my hair but doesn't actually notice that I'm sitting beside him. He is deep in a book translated by a colleague. Occasionally he nods.

My mother plays the violin in an orchestra. Scrape scrape scrape, she says when it's time to practise, and closes the door. Tomorrow she will set off to Holland.

I narrow my eyes and focus on a point in the distance. I am subtle, quick and loyal. I would have made a good ratter.

Saudade. I wonder if Gil is feeling that now for his lost friend. If he is, he is not showing any sign of it.

3

Marieka is from Sweden. Gil's mother was Portuguese-French. I need diagrams to keep track of all the nationalities in my family but I don't mind. Mongrels are wily and healthy and don't suffer displaced hips or premature madness.

My parents were over forty when they had me but I don't think of them as old, any more than they think of me as young. We are just us.

The fact that Gil's friend left home exactly when we were coming to visit is hard to understand. The police don't believe he's been murdered or kidnapped. I can imagine Gil wandering out the door and forgetting for a while to come back, but ties to Marieka and me would draw him home. Perhaps Matthew's ties are looser.

Despite being best friends, Gil and Matthew haven't seen each other in eight years. This makes the timing of his disappearance quite strange. Impolite, at the very least.

I look forward to seeing his wife and starting to understand what happened. Perhaps that's why Gil decided to take me along. Did I mention that I'm good at puzzles?

There is no need to double-check the passports; they are zipped into the inner pocket of my bag, safe, ready to be presented at check-in. Gil has put his book down and is gazing at something inside his head.

Where do you think Matthew went? I ask him.

It takes him a few seconds to return to me. He sighs and places his hand on my knee. I don't know, sweetheart.

Do you think we'll find him?

He looks thoughtful and says, Matthew was a wanderer, even as a child.

I wait to hear what he says next about his friend, but he says nothing. Inside his head he is still talking. Whole sentences flash across his eyes. I can't read them.

What? I say.

What, what? But he smiles.

What are you thinking?

Nothing important. About my childhood. I knew Matthew as well as I knew myself. When I think of him he still looks like a boy, even though he's quite old.

He's the same age as you I say, a little huffily.

Yes. He laughs, and pulls me close.

Here is the story from Gil's past:

He and Matthew are twenty-two, hitch-hiking to France in the back of a lorry with hardly any money. Then across France to Switzerland, to climb the Lauteraarhorn. Of the two, Matthew is the serious climber. It all goes according to plan until, on the second day, the temperature begins to rise. Avalanche weather. They watch the snow and ice thunder down around them. Mist descends towards evening, wrapping the mountain like a cloak. They burrow in, hoping the weather will change. Around midnight, the wind picks up and the rain turns to snow.

I've tried to imagine the scene hundreds of times. The first problem – exposure; the second – altitude. In the dead of night, in the dark and cold and wind and snow, Matthew notices the first signs of sickness in his friend and insists they descend. Gil refuses. Time passes. Head pounding, dizzy and irrational, Gil shouts, pushes Matthew off him. When at last he slumps, exhausted by the effort and the thin air, all he wants is to sit down and sleep in the snow. To die.

Over the next eleven hours, Matthew cajoles and drags and walks and talks him down the mountain. Over and over he tells Gil that you don't lie down in the snow. You keep going, no matter what.

They reach safety and Gil swears never to climb again.

And Matthew?

He was in love with it, says Gil.

He saved your life.

Gil nods.

We both fall silent, and I think, *and yet*.

And yet. Gil's life would not have needed saving if it hadn't been for Matthew.

The risk-taker and his riskee.

When I think of the way this trip has turned out, I wonder if we've been summoned for some sort of cosmic levelling, to help Matthew this time, the one who has never before required saving.

Perhaps we have been called in to balance the flow of energy in the universe.

We reach the airport. Gil picks up my bag and his, and we heave ourselves off the train. As the escalator carries us up, a text pings on to his phone.

My father is no good at texts, so he hands it to me and I show him: **Still nothing** it says, and is signed **Suzanne**. Matthew's wife.

We look at each other.

Come on, he says, piling our bags on to a trolley, and off we trot for what feels like miles to the terminal. At the check-in I ask for a window seat. Gil isn't fussy. We answer the questions about bombs and sharp objects, rummage through our carry-on bags for liquids, take our boarding passes and join the long snake through international departures. I pass the time watching other people, guessing their nationalities and relationships. American faces, I note, look unguarded. Does this make them more, or less approachable? I don't know yet.

Gil buys a newspaper and a bottle of whisky from duty-free and we go to the gate. As we board the plane I'm still thinking about that night on the mountain. What does it take to half drag, half carry a disorientated man the size of Gil, hour after hour, through freezing snow and darkness?

He may have other faults, this friend of Gil's, but he is not short of determination.

4

Suzanne meets us at international arrivals in New York. We are tired and crumpled. She spots Gil while he is trying to get his phone to work, and I nudge him and point. She's not old but looks pinched, as if someone's forgotten to water her. There is a buggy beside her and in it a child sleeps, despite all the bustle and noise. His arms stick out sideways in his padded suit. He wears a blue striped hat.

Gil kisses her and says, It's been too long. He peers down at the child. Hello, he says.

This is Gabriel, says Suzanne.

Hello, Gabriel, Gil says.

Gabriel squeezes his eyes together but doesn't wake up.

And, Mila, says Suzanne. You've changed so much.

She means that I've changed since I was four years old, when we last came to visit. That's when I met Gabriel's older brother, Owen. He was seven and I don't remember much about him, though we are holding hands in the one photo Gil has of us.

I touch the side of my finger to Gabriel's fist and he opens it and grabs on to me, still asleep. His grip is strong.

I'm sorry it's turned out like this, she says, and shakes her head. Not much fun for you. She turns to Gil. Come on. We can talk in the car.

The car is noisy and they speak in low voices so I can't catch most of what they're saying. Gabriel's in the back with me, fast asleep in his car seat. Occasionally he opens his eyes or stretches out a hand or kicks his feet, but he doesn't wake up. I make him grab on to my finger again and hear Suzanne say, Well, I hope you've made the right decision. She says it in a way that suggests he hasn't made the right decision at all, and I'm sure she's talking about bringing me along.

It has started to rain.

I fall asleep in the car to the rhythmic whoosh of wind-screen wipers and the low buzz of Gil and Suzanne talking. Normally I'd be tuning in to hear what they're saying, but I'm too tired to care. Gabriel still hangs on to my finger.

When I awake it's dark. The road is narrow and quiet, nearly deserted; the rain has stopped. I say nothing at all, just look out of the window at the woods hoping to see a deer or a bear peering at me. Gil and Suzanne have stopped talking and the car is filled with private thoughts. Suzanne's are surprisingly clear; Gil's muffled and soft. Gil will be thinking about Matthew. It's a puzzle in his head and Suzanne's and mine. Where has Matthew gone? And why?

Suzanne's thoughts sound like a CD skipping. *Damn damn damn damn damn.*

What I know already is that Matthew and Suzanne both teach at the university in town. Matthew disappeared five days ago, eight months into the academic year, fourteen months after Gabriel was born. He took nothing with him, not a change of clothing or a passport or any money. Just left for work in the morning, said goodbye as usual and never showed up to teach his class.

The actual running away does not strike me as particularly strange. Most of us are held in place by a kind of centrifugal force. If for some reason the force stopped, we might all fly off in different directions. But what about the not coming back? Staying away is frightening and painful. And who would leave a baby? Even to me this seems extreme, a failure of love.

I think hard. What would make it feel like the only thing to do?

Here are the things I come up with:

(A) Desperation (about what?)
(B) Fear (of what?)
(C) Anger (why?)

I know hardly anything about Matthew and Suzanne. I will try to find out what is what when we arrive. There are always answers. Sometimes the right answer turns out to be

(D) All of the above.

5

When Gil told me that Matthew and Suzanne lived in a wooden house in upstate New York, I pictured an old-fashioned log cabin with smoke curling out of a stone chimney, a rocking chair on the portch and hens pecking around. Their house is nothing like this. I tried to hold the original image in my head for as long as possible but it slipped away once I saw the real thing. The real thing is nothing at all like a normal house and nothing at all like a log cabin. Picture a big cube with each flat side divided into four glass squares. The roof is a big square of wood laid at an angle so the snow and rain slip off.

It is set in trees with no other houses in sight and Suzanne left the lights on when she left. When we park the car it looks like a beautiful spaceship that just happened to land in a clearing. It shimmers in the black night. In my whole life, I never saw such a beautiful house. My first thought when Suzanne turns the car engine off is that I would never run away from a house like this.

Suzanne unlocks the front door. Lying across the room is a large white Alsatian that lifts its head when we come in. Suzanne doesn't greet it. She walks straight through as if the dog does not exist. The dog seems accustomed to this and stands to move out of her way. I approach the dog and she stands perfectly still while I kneel to pat her. She has beautiful brown eyes. Loneliness flows off her in waves.

So she is Matthew's dog. The name on her tag is Honey.

Inside the house, bookcases line most of the walls and there is a huge glass-fronted stove with 'eco-burner' etched on the glass. It burns the smoke too, says Suzanne.

I wonder how it does that.

All of the bookcases have tiny lights built in, and all of the walls and ceilings too, so the house seems to twinkle.

It's so beautiful, I say to Suzanne, who is lifting Gabriel out of his padded suit. He's awake now, staring like a baby owl. He waves his hands at Honey, who watches him gravely. Suzanne points at the door. Out, she says, and Honey walks out of the room.

It was built by an architect who ran out of money, Suzanne says. It made him famous though, and now he's built another just like it, only bigger, for himself. It's called The Box House.

As we walk through the house, I collect images like a camera clicking away. I can barely remember what Matthew looks like and there are no pictures of him to remind me. No picture of him and Suzanne on their wedding day or him with Gabriel. Or just him.

Click.

Other details leap out at me: A pair of muddy shoes. A stack of bills. A cracked window. A closed door. A pile of clothes. A skateboard. A dog. *Click click click.*

First impressions? This is not a happy house.

6

My best friend in London is called Catlin. She has hair like straw and thin arms and legs, and starting from when we were seven or eight we always went to her house after school, partly because it was on the way to mine and partly because the top floor has a hidden passageway under the roof through a door at the back of an old cupboard. Perfect for a clubhouse.

We designed code books and stashed our pocket money in a box under the floorboards, making plans to hide out when the enemy invaded Camden. Catlin was big on logistics so we spent days drawing maps of underground escape tunnels running all through London, connecting to sewers and ghost tube stations.

All the people we knew were rated according to how much of a security risk they'd turn out to be when things turned bad. Cat and I had top security clearance and were Head of State and Head of Security respectively. Gil was Senior Codebreaker with four-star clearance. Marieka would be Chief of Operations. Five star.

Catlin's parents were more of a problem. Her father shouted a lot, worked most of the time and was best avoided on the occasions he appeared at home. He and her mother rarely spoke. We made them Protocol Officers, a mysterious title, with only three-star clearance. I thought Cat might be offended that her parents had less trustworthy rankings than mine but she didn't seem to mind.

One day on the way to school Catlin said in her casual voice, My parents don't like each other. She looked at me, watching my reaction.

Lots of parents don't, I said, because I didn't want to hurt her feelings.

They're probably getting a divorce, she said.

I thought she might be crying because she sounded strange, but when I turned to look she was crouching down with an insane grin on her face and then she launched herself straight up into the air like a spring, shouting, I HATE THEM! with something like glee.

For a smallish person she has a very loud voice.

Shouting seemed to make her feel better, though I doubted what she said was true. Most people don't actually hate their parents, even if they are horrible. Her mother, at least, isn't horrible. She always brought biscuits and drinks on a tray up to the top floor where we were planning for the invasion. She never knocked, just quietly left it next to the cupboard door. I liked her for that, though she always seemed a bit sleepwalkerish. The house as a whole felt dulled, as if some-one had sucked all the colour out with a straw. I wondered if Catlin noticed that it was different from other houses or whether it just looked normal to her.

This year, for the first time, Catlin and I stopped being in the same class together. She was suddenly wild and loud – rolling her school skirt up short and hanging out with older boys, the ones who scare old people on buses by swearing and smoking cigarettes. It was weird not to walk home with her every day but eventually I got used to it. Sometimes, walking past her house, I had to stop myself turning up the path out of habit.

It wasn't exactly like we avoided each other, and I didn't exactly miss her because she seemed like someone I no longer knew. But every single day I missed the person who used to be my friend. The worst was once when our eyes met by accident and she looked away.

Then, on the last day of spring term, she ran up behind me and shouted *Boom!* like in the old days and we ended up walking home together, pretending everything was normal.

Oh my god, Catlin said, eyes huge. Did you see Miss Evans as the Easter bunny?

Miss Evans is one of our PE teachers. She's a genuine freak, never missing a chance to dress up as Father Christmas or Karl Marx or Harry Potter.

Très awkward, I said.

Très très awkward!! She danced around me, hands fluttering like a joke ballerina.

We fell back in step again.

Are you around over Easter? Her tone was casual, her head almost in her schoolbag as she rummaged around for a lipstick.

The question was surprising because what about her new gang of cool friends? I have to go to New York, I told her. We're visiting an old friend of my dad's.

She didn't answer and it made me feel like apologizing

for going away, which was ridiculous as she'd barely spoken to me for months.

We got to her house and she didn't even say goodbye, just turned and ran up the path like she was angry, and I wondered if it was because I was going away and she wasn't, or because maybe she wanted to be friends again when it wasn't a convenient time for me.

Hey, Cat! I called after her. I'll let you know what America's like! But she was halfway through the door and didn't even turn round.

I stared at the door as it slammed and just as I was leaving I saw her disembodied face peering back at me through the window. Then both her hands crept up into the window like they belonged to someone else and she made a horrible face and started strangling herself, stuck out her tongue, went cross-eyed and disappeared down the bottom of the window.

Bye! I shouted again and waved.

A minute later I got a text from her. It said: **bring me back an American Easter egg**

And I answered: **save me a London one**

And she wrote back: **OK**

And I wrote back: **OK**

And she wrote back: **make it a big one**

And I wrote back: **ditto**

And we both felt better.

7

I am dizzy and a little sick with jet lag. Suzanne puts me in a small room off the study with a built-in bed. One end of my bed is a glass wall that faces out into the woods. She shows me how to use the blinds but I leave them open. I am so tired that I don't remember falling asleep, and a minute later it is noon the next day. Trees break the light up into fragments; above them, the sky is blue and clear. It couldn't be more different from our view in London, which is mainly of other houses.

Gil brings me milky coffee in bed. He smiles but looks distracted. Now that I am fully awake I scan the room – a small desk, a metal swivel chair, two pairs of trainers neatly placed in a corner. A bookshelf holds the *Guinness Book of Records* from a few years ago, a US Army Survival Manual, an ancient copy of *Treasure Island* with a worn leather cover, a tall pile of school notebooks and sports magazines. Just above is a shelf on which silver swimming trophies stand side by side and I realize with a start that this is Owen's room. There's a picture of him with Suzanne in a silver frame. He's got his arm round her shoulders and is already a few inches taller. The room has been tidied and dusted, but a set of keys, a birthday card and a bowl of coins still sit on the dresser as if he will come along any minute to claim them.

Gil clocks the direction of my gaze. Come and have breakfast when you're ready, he says. Did you sleep well?

I nod. Did you?

He shrugs. Honey appears round the corner, silent as a ghost. I put out my hand and she licks it.

No news? I ask, and he shakes his head.

Are we going to look for him?

I have to think, Gil says. Possibly.

I want to say, What if he's been murdered? Or jumped in front of a train? But I don't. Gil would have thought of that, anyway. He must think it hasn't happened. I suppose he might be keeping up appearances, pretending he thinks his friend is still alive so as not to upset me, but I doubt it. My father's faults involve excessive honesty. And absent-mindedness, of course.

Where do you think he went? What if we can't find him? Will he let us know he's OK?

Perguntador. My father pronounces the word with a slight smile. It is Portuguese for someone who asks too many questions, and he's used the word as a nickname for me for as long as I can remember. First things first, he says. Drink your coffee. Have a shower. Get dressed. Come down to breakfast – He looks at his watch – lunch. We'll talk to Suzanne and make a plan. OK?

OK. I dig clean clothes out of my suitcase and take the towel from beside my bed. Honey watches me gravely. She is like a lost dog only she's not the one who's lost.

I take out my phone, snap a picture and text it to Catlin. **Lots of trees in New York.**

And she texts back: **Shd be tall buildings. Sure ur in the right place?**

It's called upstate I tell her.

There's a pause, then another bleep.

Got my egg yet?

Not yet I text back.

ok.

I put my phone down on a shelf in the shower room, which is black slate – walls, ceiling and floor. Once I figure out how it works, I want to stand under the hot water all day. The soap Suzanne put out for me is also black, and smells of coconut. I make a thick lather and watch it slide down the drain. When I turn the water off, the room is so full of steam it's like standing in a cloud. I wrap myself in the dark-green towel, pine green, the same colour as the trees outside the house. Despite the seriousness of our mission, I am, for this moment, perfectly content.

There is toast for breakfast, and no sign of Suzanne. Gil says she's gone to work for an hour or so, and we can make ourselves at home till she comes back. Gabriel's babysitter has taken him to playgroup.

What do you think? he asks, looking at me carefully.

Sometimes I observe things I can't interpret. Like two people smiling and holding hands when actually they hate each other. This confuses me, and Gil says that's because it is, in actual fact, confusing. It's the same with being a translator. Some things can't be translated because the words don't exist in the other language, or the meaning is so entirely

22

specific to one place or one way of speaking that it disappears in translation.

But sometimes there are clues.

The house, I say a little tentatively, is beautiful.

And?

I take a deep breath. Suzanne is a very tidy person. All her things and Gabriel's are put away. But she hasn't touched *his* things. Look . . .

Gil looks.

A sweater crumpled on the floor. Muddy boots, shoved in a corner. A pile of mail, stacked on a table. It's almost –

He waits.

– as if they live in two separate houses that don't touch. Like . . . only one of them is vegetarian, I say, pointing to the shelf of cookbooks.

That's not uncommon.

I look at him, not knowing whether it's common or uncommon. I just know what a family in which everyone gets along feels like, with all the edges of things blurred and overlapping. What I feel in this house is containment. Suzanne containing her things so they don't touch his. Even the baby doesn't seem to cross over, his toys and clothes and equipment all tidy and stacked up on her plane.

And she hates his dog.

I don't say it, but I've felt other things. Owen, for instance. I can feel him all through the house. They pretend he's gone, but he's everywhere, like a restless soul.

There's someone else. A smoker. Suzanne has a friend who smokes. There are traces of smoke in her clothes, in her hair. And more. I can smell it in certain parts of the house, which suggests it's not just someone she knows, but someone who spends time here. And it's definitely a man. Women smell of things other than themselves – hair stuff, shampoo, soap – even if they don't wear perfume.

Does Matthew smoke? I ask.

Never, Gil says, looking puzzled. Couldn't stand the idea. Why?

I shrug.

Gil sips his coffee. Suzanne says Matthew has a camp near the Canadian border.

When I look puzzled, he says, A little house. Like a shack.

Matthew has a camp. Not *we* have a camp.

She wonders if he's gone there. Gil looks at me over the rim of his cup. It's quite isolated. In the woods. The sort of place used by hunters.

Hunters?

Gil smiles. Matthew doesn't hunt. But maybe we should go and have a look. It's the obvious place for him to hide. Suzanne says she'll stay here with Gabriel in case he comes back.

I think for a minute. Is it normal for people just to disappear? I ask.

Normal? Gil raises an eyebrow. Not really. No such thing as normal, Perguntador.

No such thing as normal. Gil's favourite line. I finish my toast and look out at the trees, just coming into leaf. I have learned normal as a word with no real meaning in our language, but sometimes I wonder what it would feel like.

What time is it in Holland? I ask him. Can we phone Marieka?

24

Yes, Gil says, and we do, but she's out so we leave a message. I flop down on the comfortable sofa and when I open my eyes Honey is standing a few inches away just looking at me. I sigh, get up and find her lead, and we go out together for a walk in the woods behind the house. I don't go far because I don't want to get lost.

Matthew's dog is a watcher, like me. Her eyes have a sadness that is almost human. She wants to know who I am. She follows me and pricks her ears to listen when I speak. Perhaps she is hoping I will explain things to her, where Matthew went and when he will be back, but I do not know the answers to these questions, and besides, I do not speak dog.

Honey is intelligent and loyal.

I wonder how Suzanne can hate such a dog.

8

You'd never think of matching Catlin and me up as friends. She's loud, skinny as a twig and pretty much bonkers. I'm quiet, solid and think things through. Cat always jumps first, before she has time to be swayed by facts. While I'm cautious. But I love how bright and daring she is, like a shooting star. She's not like anyone else I've ever met, and sometimes I wonder why she's friends with me.

Once she dragged me upstairs to our clubhouse to look at a cardboard box. Inside were two rats.

I stared at her.

Two rats had gone missing from the school science lab the week before and everyone was hysterical because they were at large. Some people wouldn't even use the school toilets in case they bobbed up in the water underneath them, which apparently happens.

You're a *rat-napper*? I was appalled. How'd you get them out of the building?

Cat pointed at her feet, grinning.

What? I said. You stuffed them in your *shoes*?

Almost. And then she reached down and picked up one of the rats and slipped her hand and the rat into a sock, removed her hand, tied the sock loosely at the end, and voilà, it was the perfect rat carrier. Being schoolroom rats, they were overfed and a bit dopey and docile from being passed around, so inside the dark sock they just curled up and dozed.

Where'd you learn that trick?

Made it up, she said, which figured. Most of what Cat tells me she makes up, but she's so entertaining, it doesn't matter. I prefer her explanations to the real ones anyway.

Her plan was for us to train the rats to carry messages through the sewers – though what messages and to whom was kind of up for grabs.

We weren't allowed to name them, she said, because then we'd get attached, which was extremely unprofessional. So they became Rat One and Rat Two. The first time I picked up Rat One, he scooted up my arm and scrambled down into my shirt.

The next day when two girls jumped up on chairs in the science lab screaming that they'd seen a rat, I didn't even turn round, just said not to bother, there were no rats. Everyone stared at me suspiciously, thinking, *How does she know?*

Anyway, on Tuesday we fed the rats cheese and biscuits and bits of sausage and grass, but by the time we got home from school on Wednesday they had chewed through the cardboard box and were gone.

We never saw them again. Catlin's mum kept complaining that she heard chewing in the cupboards at night, and her dad said, Don't be stupid you must be imagining things, and apparently there were big fights, though in that family there were always big fights. Cat said she thought the escaped rats were the straw that broke the camel's back between her parents, i.e., they ruined their marriage once and for all. There was no way I could tell her that she was wrong, that it was obvious from the first time you met her parents that they just didn't like each other and would have got divorced sooner or later, rats or no rats.

It must be horrible to realize that you come from two people who never should have got together in the first place.

After the rat incident, we started spending more time at my house where everyone got along and there was no shouting. Looking back, I wonder if that was one of the reasons we stopped being friends.

One time when we had to go back to her house after school, we found her mum out and everything perfectly tidy and all the windows in the house closed up tight, despite the fact that it was a beautiful spring day. It was cold and grey inside, like no one had told the house that winter was over. And outside, trees floated with blossom and birds sang.

We picked up our code books from the clubhouse even though we didn't play spies much any more, and we didn't even bother checking the fridge. We just wanted to get out of there.

Mum doesn't hear rats any more, Cat said. They've deserted us, like a sinking ship.

She looked downcast, so I squeaked *Avast ye hearties!* and *Mizzen ye swarthy poop deck!* and we slammed the door and ran back to mine, shouting in pig-pirate all the way. And when we arrived, Gil called hello from his study, Marieka showed up with bunches of asparagus, and you could smell hyacinths through the windows. At the time I thought it was nice but maybe Cat hated it.

The following year, when we weren't speaking, it occurred to me that her new personality actually made sense – that kissing boys and smoking weed and stomping out of class and insulting teachers and generally acting about a hundred times worse and louder than you really are is what you might do in order not to think about having to go home to sleep in that sad grey house.

9

Translating books is an odd way to make a living. It is customary to translate from your second language into your first, but among my father's many friends and colleagues, every possible combination of language and direction is represented.

Gil translates from Portuguese into English. Most translators grow up speaking two or three languages but some speak a ridiculous number; the most I've heard is twelve. They say it gets easier after the first three or four.

The people I find disturbing are those with no native language at all. Gil's friend Nicholas had a French mother and a Dutch father. At home he spoke French, Dutch and English but he grew up in Switzerland speaking Italian and German at school. When I ask him which language he thinks in, he says, Depends what I'm thinking about.

The idea of having no native language worries me. Would you feel like a nomad inside your own head? I can't imagine having no words that are home. A language orphan.

Perhaps this worries me because it is not a million miles away from my reality. Marieka grew up speaking Swedish first, then English; Gil learned Portuguese, French and

English as a child. I can understand conversations in most of these languages, but the only one I speak properly is my own.

Marieka rolls her eyes when Gil tries to explain syntactic semiotics or tells us his theory of typologies over breakfast. His grandad was a miner, his father became a teacher, but Gil trumped them all with a PhD in applied linguistics. Remember your roots, Mum says, and hmphs. Semiotics!

I love to hear Gil talk but don't always pay attention to the words. When I do listen, I rarely know what he's talking about, but neither of us really minds. Sometimes it puzzles me that he's my father, given how differently our minds work. Perhaps I was switched at birth and my real father is Hercule Poirot.

Marieka's mother was Swedish-Sudanese and though she's fair-skinned like her father, she has beautiful red and gold hair, like a shrub on fire. Gil says he was first attracted to Mum's hair and only afterwards listened to her playing. It was a concert his friend dragged him to and he spent the first half thinking about a paper he was writing and only looked up after the interval to see this woman with wild curls playing the violin.

Marieka couldn't believe anyone would come backstage and appear not even to have noticed the music. She's used to it now, but at the time thought he was eccentric, possibly mad.

I once asked my parents why they didn't live together for the first eight years and Gil just said, We were happy as we were.

He says he never thought of another woman, not even

once, after he met Marieka, and then in the same sentence says, Do you think I'll need my grey suit in Geneva? and Marieka smiles and says, Yes, my darling, you'll probably need it.

Marieka notices the world in what she calls a Scandinavian way, which means without a lot of drama. I register every emotion, every relationship, every subtext. If someone is angry or sad or disappointed, I see it like a neon sign. There's no way to explain how, I just do. For a long time I thought everyone did.

That poor man, I'd say, and Marieka would look puzzled.

Look! I'd say. Look how he stands, the way his mouth twists, how his eyes move around the room. Look at his shoulders, the way his jacket fits, how he clutches his book. Look at his shoes. The way he licks his lips.

The impression was so clear – a great drift of hovering facts – it amazed me that she couldn't see it. But Gil says human capacities are vast and varied. He doesn't understand how people can speak just one language. Certain combinations of chords make Marieka wince. I peer into souls.

Of course, most people don't pay attention. They barge into a situation and start asking questions when the answers are already there.

Where's Marieka? for instance. Gil's favourite.

I look at him. What day is it? Which fiddle has she taken? Which shoes?

Three simple observations tell me instantly where she is and how long she'll be gone. But Gil always asks. Flat shoes, I tell him. Because of the stairs. There are five flights of stairs up to the place where she practises quartets. Otherwise she nearly always wears heels because she likes to be tall. And if you manage to miss the shoes, the baroque violin is gone.

Sometimes I go along with Marieka because they rehearse in the viola player's tiny flat at the top of an old building in Covent Garden, with long windows looking out across London. If I lie on the floor and rest my chin on my hands, my eyes reach just over the narrow skirting board and I can pretend I'm in a balloon floating over Covent Garden. I took Catlin along once but she couldn't keep quiet.

When we first heard that Matthew had disappeared, Marieka and Gil had a long conversation about what to do.

What if it's *not* fairly straightforward? Marieka asked. And Gil answered in a murmuring voice that I couldn't hear.

I don't want Mila mixed up with that mumblemumble family and you know what I buzzbuzz about Suzanne.

Well, I do happen to know what she buzzbuzzes about Suzanne. She doesn't much like her, though she also says it's hard to be likeable when you're so unhappy. But Marieka knew Suzanne before Owen died, and says that even then she never seemed to be telling the truth. I wonder why I haven't seen Suzanne since I was four. Gil says he and Matthew are like brothers, but when did they last meet? Are they like brothers who have grown apart?

What do you think? asks Marieka. I can't hear the answer, but I know my father well enough to imagine what he'd say. Matthew just gets like this sometimes. I'm sure it's nothing serious. We'll go over as planned. He'll be home by the time we arrive. He *is* my oldest friend. And in any case, it's been much too long since I've seen him. Perhaps I can mumble bumble fumble tumble humph.

33

I have heard stories of the two of them as boys hanging out in the cemetery behind their school, talking about girls and drinking themselves unconscious on cider. I've seen pictures, long before Gil and Marieka met, of the two young men brown from the sun and grinning in Spain, Scotland, the Alps. In pictures they look handsome and young, their friendship tested only briefly by a girl they both loved. In one photo both of them have an arm round her but her head is turned and she's smiling at Matthew, who looks straight into the camera. Gil's face is in shadow.

Once when his mother was ill, Matthew lived with Gil's family for a whole year. He and Gil shared a room, staying up half the night reading comics Matthew stole from the local shop.

Stole?

Matthew, Gil says, not me.

What happened to his mother?

She died, Perguntador. The summer he was fifteen.

I would like to have known them back then, though I suspect that Gil young wouldn't be all that different from Gil not-young. I have heard how they sat next to each other during the eleven-plus and later their A-levels – Matthew clever at history, Gil at languages, both offered places at Cambridge.

Two grammar school boys from the fag end of Preston, Gil says. On the day the news came we felt like gods.

Gil used summers to study and write. Matthew hitch-hiked round the Black Sea, climbed Annapurna, taught English in East Africa.

*

34

Marieka phones back. She sounds the same as always on the phone.

Hmm, is what she says now, when I tell her about cute baby Gabriel and Honey and the feeling in the beautiful glass house. And then she sighs, and says, Do be careful, my darling, families can be so complicated.

I tell her I will be careful, and that I love her, and then I give the phone to Gil. His whole body uncurls when he speaks to her.

For a minute I feel like crying because I miss Marieka, but then I see her in my head saying, Do you imagine I'm not with you, silly?

We are three. Even when we are just two, we are three.

10

Catlin always talked about running away, but not in the usual way where you seek out your real parents who are rich and glamorous and gave you up for adoption by mistake and have regretted it ever since.

She wanted to run away to Brussels or Washington DC and head up an international spy ring that would save the world from mass destruction, preferably at the very last second. This she would accomplish by writing an impossibly elaborate computer program involving twenty-eight prime numbers coded into one uniquely high-spec iPhone. I tend to drift off when she talks tech.

All of our spy games involved threats to the free world and invasion by evil enemies while we plotted routes through underground tunnels known to no one but us thanks to a map Cat discovered in the catacombs under the British Museum in an ancient box sealed with a curse.

Untouched for two hundred years, Cat said. Feast your eyes, matey.

I feasted my eyes on an ancient-looking folder, scarred and burnt round the edges, and even though I knew she'd used an old iron to burn the edges and make a bit of ordinary bit of card look antique, I was impressed. It did look old.

Wow, I said, reaching for it. But she pushed my hand away and made me put on bright blue washing-up gloves, which had a satisfying forensic appearance when used out of context. With my gloves on, I was allowed to hold the file while Cat dusted it with baby powder for fingerprints.

Just as I thought, she said with a mad gleam in her eye. Last handled by foreign operatives.

Really? How can you tell? I was genuinely curious.

Look closely, she whispered. See how the fingerprint whirlygigs go backwards? That's foreign.

I must have looked sceptical because Cat bristled. Fine, don't believe me. You think I care?

I believe you, I said.

As you should, young Mila. As you should.

And the date? I asked. I didn't want to piss her off again.

She held one of the pieces of burnt paper from the file up to the bare light bulb in the clubhouse. As I thought, she said. It's ninety per cent linen, distinct greenish hue (that was from the walls in the clubhouse, which were painted green and gave us a greenish hue too), made in Czechoslovania between . . . hmm . . . 1918 and 1920.

You had to give the girl credit.

And then she carefully looked at all the information in our file, while I drew an approximation of a stencil in red pencil at the top of every page:

TOP SECRET

If we'd managed to hang on to the rats, we could have tied coded notes to their legs, but instead we worked on innocuous-sounding phrases for our code books that would allow us to exchange vital information in public. When I say we worked on phrases, what I mean is that Cat made them up and I said they were good. Here are some examples:

Take an umbrella = TRUST NO ONE
I'm thirsty = I HAVE NEWS
What's for dinner? = WE'VE BEEN BETRAYED
Nice curtains = WE'RE DOOMED

If I ever suggested a phrase, Cat would think of a reason why it wasn't quite right, so after a while I stopped bothering. I didn't mind though, just continued on with my TOP SECRET lettering, which got more and more professional-looking until you might have thought we had a real stamp.

Are you getting a picture of our relationship? The thing is, I could have chosen a more straightforward friend, but I didn't. It never really occurred to me that the friends you choose reveal you. Take Matthew and Gil. Gil required a leader and Matthew a follower. With Cat and me, I was the anchor. I would never, for instance, stuff rats into socks. But Cat was the spark.

It was all good fun, except that I never got to be the one who made the twenty-eight digit prime number code to save the world, despite understanding prime numbers far better than Cat did. She thought you could just have a mystical feeling about a number, no matter how many times I told her that 'prime' meant not being divisible by anything. To Catlin, thirty-nine was a prime number because it looked sinister. Despite it totally not being one.

As for her elaborate save-the-world fantasy – well, maybe it wasn't a random choice. I would rather have played something else occasionally, like orphans or explorers or hospitals. But if my family had been like hers, I might have been equally desperate to come up with the right combination of prime numbers to make the world safe again.

11

Gabriel and his babysitter are back from playgroup. Her name is Caryn, C-a-r-y-n in case we were thinking of going with the usual spelling, and she looks uneasy when we tell her that Suzanne isn't home yet but it's all right, she can go. She says, No, it's OK, I'll just fix his boddle in case Mommy's delayed.

But Mommy isn't delayed, she's back, still looking stressed, but happy to see Gabriel and also – though somewhat less so – us. She asks if I like DVDs and gives me a choice of *Titanic* or *Amélie*. I don't really care, but choose *Amélie*. I start to watch the movie and it's fine, but I want to know what Suzanne and Gil are talking about more than I want to watch Amélie save the world.

Gil says, What else? And Suzanne answers with a sigh.

Maybe he's having an affair with one of his students. I don't know.

And then I am inside the head of a person with a young child whose husband has gone missing and I am much more upset and panicked than Suzanne. What if he's *dead*? screams this person with a child. What if I *never see him again*?

But nothing about Suzanne is screaming. When I say this

to Gil, he nods as if he's noticed the same thing. I suspect there's more to this marriage than we know, he says. And of course Owen changed everything. Most couples who lose a child don't stay together.

I've been thinking about the connection between language and thought. Languages that read from left to right picture the passage of time moving left to right. If a French speaker tells the story of a cat catching a mouse, time starts at the left and moves to the right. Hebrew and Arabic speakers start with the cat and the mouse on the right and time passes to the left. So it's not just a question of words.

I try to remember this when I talk to Suzanne, and wonder how time moves in her brain. Maybe it stopped when Owen died. Or got dammed up like logs in a stream. Or just goes round and round like the clock icon on a computer. Whatever it is, she seems like a person made of glass. Tap her and she'll shatter into a billion pieces.

It is difficult having a conversation with a glass person but she watches patiently when I hold Gabriel and feed him his boddle, even though I can tell she wants him back. Honey desperately wants to protect the baby. She makes a faint noise in her throat and Suzanne shoos her away. Suzanne is not a horrible person masquerading as a nice one, just an angry one pretending to be normal.

Perhaps she is the sort of person who says nothing for fear of exploding with words. In my presence, at least, she doesn't ever mention Matthew. The language that structures her thoughts seems to be one that no one else speaks. And she avoids the only other creature who shares her loss. I think the dog's unhappiness frightens her.

Gabriel is too young to notice. I play a game with him where I lower a toy mouse on a string over his face and jerk it up again. He laughs and laughs and then out of nowhere his face collapses and he starts to howl. Suzanne swoops in and picks him up, saying, Mommy's here. Gil looks at me.

I walk over to the thousands of books displayed on the walls, run my hand along them and pick one out; *Caravanserai*, it's called. Camels. Women draped in black. Men squatting, drinking tiny cups of tea. Low square buildings decorated with inscriptions I can't read. It looks hot and quiet and slow.

Between jet lag and the oddness of being without street noise and other people, the afternoon passes.

Suzanne is going into town for a few things and asks if I'd like to come. Yes, please, I say, and we take Gabriel along too. Gil stays put. He'll work.

On the fifteen-minute drive Suzanne asks me all the usual questions about how I like school and how is my mother, and where is she performing these days, etc. It is polite adult talk and only just lacks the genuine curiosity that connects people.

Suzanne apologizes for the supermarket being boring but I don't find it boring at all. To me it's almost as exotic as *Caravanserai*. She says to tell her if I see anything I'd like to buy.

I see lots of things I'd like to buy: macaroni and cheese in a box, plasters with cartoons of superheroes on them, peanut butter and marshmallow swirled round in a huge plastic jar. In the bakery department there are cakes with talking clown heads and musical merry-go-round ponies in bright colours. The breakfast cereal section goes on for half a mile and I wonder how anyone ever chooses. I'm looking for Easter eggs but the ones I find are all too ugly or too childish or too similar to the ones I could buy at home. When at last I catch up with Suzanne she's talking on the phone. Her face looks different from the one Gil and I have seen. It's younger, suddenly, and her smile is one she has not shown us.

I approach her through the fruit section, where watermelons, apples and bananas all look twice the size of the ones in England. How can this be?

When she sees me she says, I have to go, and clicks off. Her smile has gone all pink and sugary like the clown head on the cake. A friend from book club, she explains, unnecessarily.

A friend? I don't hate Suzanne but I can't bring myself to like her either. She's one of those people who thinks that because I'm young I'm blind to what's true and what's not. I see her far more clearly than she sees me, perhaps more clearly than she sees herself.

Suzanne has to go to the dry-cleaner and the post office, so we pile the groceries into the back of the car and she says, If you'd like to walk around a bit on your own, feel free. Just meet us here in half an hour.

I wander off to a sports shop and browse the T-shirts, but there's nothing I want to buy and anyway I don't have any dollars. Across the road there's a bench catching the last bit of sun and I sit down.

Hey Cat, I text. **Wish u wuz here.**

I wait for a while but Catlin doesn't answer. In the meantime, everyone's running around like crazy, and it's funny to think that rush hour exists in a town the size of a peanut as well as at home. I sit as still as humanly possible, making myself invisible so I can watch what's going on without being seen. It works. No one looks.

The only thing worth watching is a man who backs his 4x4 much too fast into a parking spot and smashes the car behind him by mistake. He shouts at his kid, who's maybe sixteen, for distracting him, and the kid gets out of the car, slams the door and storms off while the guy gets down on his knees to examine the dent in the other car.

Catlin texts back. **Me too. It rains.** Attached is what I think might be a photo of a puddle. It's hard to tell.

I tear myself away from the local five-star entertainment to meet Suzanne at the car. Gabriel stares at me intently and when I smile at him his entire face lights up.

We drive back to the house without saying much. Suzanne talks to Gabriel, who's grizzling in the back seat. Who's Mommy's tired boy, she says, and then glances over at me like we're in a conspiracy. Being with her makes me tired. Then I remember Owen and feel ashamed.

Dinner is risotto with peas and Parmesan cheese. It tastes nice but halfway through the meal I excuse myself to lie on the sofa. Honey is beside me on the floor. I close my eyes and rest one hand on her back, feeling the rise and fall of her slow breathing. Gil covers me with a blanket. He thinks I'm asleep.

So, he says in a low voice, sitting back down at the table. What are we going to do?

Suzanne doesn't answer right away. Eventually she says, I can't leave. Surely you can see that. I can't leave Gabriel and my students and . . . everything.

I hear Gil sigh. Suzanne, tell me please. There must be more.

There is a silence. I can almost hear the fizzing of Suzanne's nerves.

Tell me, he says.

She begins to speak, quietly, so I have to strain to hear. I don't know, she says. He says he's fine but he's not. He blames himself for Owen. Her laugh is bitter. I blame him too. I hoped Gabriel might make it better, but surprise, surprise, it's worse. So it's true what everyone says about save-the-marriage babies. Who'd have guessed?

Gil says my name. He was not born yesterday. I make a noise like a sleeping person, a kind of grumbly sigh. It works. I was not born yesterday either.

And?

Who the hell knows? He doesn't speak much, your friend.

My father doesn't speak much either. He uses words sparingly, as if they're rationed. It's what comes, I think, of knowing so many words in so many languages. Too much choice.

You knew that when you married him. Gil speaks gently, without reproach.

Yes, of course. But knowing it, and then living for sixteen years with a man who doesn't speak . . . it's different, surely?

There is an edge to her voice, like a knife. For the first time I realize how much older Matthew must be than Suzanne. If Matthew is Gil's age, he's nearing sixty. And if Suzanne's just had a baby, can she be much more than forty?

Marieka always says fondly that she has to read Gil's mind. I've become very good at it, says she. And then she

45

kisses him on the back of the neck if he is bent over his work, and he reaches up one hand and buries his fingers in her thick hair and she turns her head and kisses his wrist. There is something in this gesture that makes me feel completely safe. Despite the fact that the scene does not include me, it does not exclude me either.

I feel a sudden rush of pity for Gabriel with his glass mother, his glass house, his baby smile.

Take the car, please, Suzanne is saying. I don't need it. I have a friend nearby; she can take me to college.

She? I think. Whoever visits isn't a she.

I close my eyes once more and when I open them again I realize that time has passed and the conversation has moved on. *What have I missed?*

It's late, Gil says. Goodnight, Suzanne.

I don't have to pretend to be woozy now. I lean on Gil till we get to my room and he folds back the covers of my bed. That's all I remember.

12

In the morning, Gil says we're going on a road trip. He says it almost gaily; we are both keen to move on. There doesn't seem to be enough air in this house, though I don't know how that can be.

I'll miss Gabriel. He claps his hands now when he sees me or I call his name, and he snuggles into my shoulder when I pick him up. I like the feel of him, compact and much heavier than he looks. Like a bundle. I've never known a baby as a person and now I can see why people like them. When he looks at me and smiles I feel chosen.

Gabriel B-B-Billington, I sing. Gabriel B-B-Billington! Gabriel giggles and waves his hands. Do you think he knows his name? I ask Suzanne.

Of course. She smiles. He'll miss you when you go.

Do you think he misses his dad? I look at her.

Suzanne's mouth pulls up tighter than ever. Does his dad miss him? That would be my question.

I must look a little shocked because she reaches out and touches my elbow softly. Don't worry, Mila. Everything will work out in the end. She pushes her hair back off her face with a tired gesture and I think, what end? The end of time?

After a minute I say, Do you want Matthew to come back?

Suzanne frowns. Yes, of course I want him to come back. She glances at Gabriel, then back at me. How could I not?

As answers go, this is not the same as saying, Oh my, yes, if only god would send him home tomorrow I would die happy. It's closer to: Do I want him back? Not especially. But if he happened to come home I'd certainly be happy for Gabriel.

Gabriel's much too little to understand any of this. I guess he'll get the picture someday, but I hope it's not soon. I've only known him for one day but already I feel protective of him. If you could see his big fat smiley face and his little pursed-up birdie mouth, you'd feel the same. I find it hard to believe that a person could walk away from that face.

Suzanne's phone rings and I carry Gabriel into the living room and plunk him on the sofa. I throw a squashy yellow ball at him and he flaps at it with his hands. Flap flap flap. He's no good at catching but I don't want to make him feel bad so I take the ball and throw it again. Flap flap flap flap-flapflap!!! He makes a high squeaking noise like a bat. Gil is standing behind me, watching.

He's very endearing.

He is, I say. He makes you love him. I throw the ball again and he flips and flaps but I can see that his face is starting to screw up like last time so we stop playing ball and I snuggle him into the corner of the squashy sofa on my lap and jiggle him and sing him a song and he calms down and doesn't scream again.

I wouldn't leave him, I say.

Gil shrugs a little and frowns and doesn't say *There's nowt so queer as folk*, which is another of his favourite expressions and probably one he doesn't particularly want to apply to his oldest friend, it being not very flattering. He doesn't look happy.

What are the possibilities? I speak quietly because I can still hear Suzanne on the phone in the next room. She has quite a bright voice on – maybe it's someone at the university or a neighbour she doesn't know very well. She even laughs a little to show that she's OK, but it doesn't have that effect.

I suppose he might have got mixed up in something he shouldn't have.

Like?

Like bad company.

What sort of bad company? For an instant I imagine something like the gas company, only full of villains.

Gil shrugs again. Drugs? Gambling? He raises an eyebrow. Smuggling, prostitution, contraband, arms trading, money laundering.

My expression makes him laugh.

Well, you asked. And no, I don't actually think Matt is running a prostitution ring. Not his style. Or at least it never was before. People do change, I suppose. Or something happens so you don't recognize them any more. It happens.

A wave of anxiety chokes me and I think of Catlin. I know it happens. The possibility that someone I know well can all of a sudden change makes me feel sick. I pull Gabriel close and kiss him so Gil won't see how I feel.

Though more usually it's the other way round, Gil continues. More usually you don't see someone for thirty

49

years and when you meet up again it's exactly the way it was back then.

He thinks for a minute, and then says, Matt's had a bad time. It probably goes back to Owen, but what do I know? Maybe it's not that at all. Maybe he's gay and living a lie. I've known him a very long time, he says. But you never really know what's going on in someone else's head. There's nowt so queer as folk, he says.

I manage a smile and Gil looks up and blinks, as if he's forgotten I'm here. And that's the end of today's lecture, he says, as Suzanne comes back in, staring at her phone accusingly.

What lecture? she asks, but it sounds more automatic than curious.

I'm still snuggled up with Gabriel but when he sees his mum he begins flapping his hands and making his high-pitched bat noise. Suzanne's phone rings again. She looks at the number, answers it, and her voice changes once more. Let me phone you back, she says, and turns her attention to Gabriel, sweeping him up out of my lap.

Pooh! she says, giving an exaggerated sniff. Smelly boy! And she's off to change his nappy.

I have the nose of a bloodhound and he didn't smell of anything but baby.

Let's hit the road, Dad says. It's getting late.

13

Fluency in two languages does not make you a translator. And translators from French to German (for instance) rarely translate from German back to French. It's a one-way process, Gil says.

He also says the trick is to visualize the rhythms and idiom of Language One in Language Two – to find the connections between, say, a German mind and a French mind, so that the peculiarities of one voice can be teased into the other without a *calamitous loss of meaning*. Which he always says in italics.

Today, I will be translating from American to English and back again, which should be just about manageable.

We set off at last, after Suzanne phones the insurance company twice to check that her policy covers any driver, including a foreign one. She spends a long time talking to Gil about the cabin Matthew owns near the Canadian border. No phone, no electricity, no running water. No Internet. She gives us a map with the route and our destination marked in red pen. We have GPS, she says, but it gets blinky up there. Best to have the map. Matt doesn't believe in GPS, she adds, as if he'll be with us on the way, disapproving of our methods.

On the other side of the map is a list of phone numbers, including hers, Matthew's mobile and the Automobile Association of America in case of an accident. She's a very organized person, is Suzanne.

The cabin, she says, is the only place I can imagine him going. Not that my imagination is anything to go by. The drive should take about seven hours. Depends on traffic. Crazy to do it in one day, and what if you get all the way there and it's shut up and empty? This route, she says, running her finger up along a long thin lake, won't add much to your journey but is nicer.

So we're hunting down a missing person via the scenic route? Tempting though it is, I don't say this out loud.

You've come all this way, she says. At least don't spend your entire time on the thruway.

OK, Gil says. Don't worry about us. We're good at maps.

The expression on Suzanne's face makes me think she's anxious, but not about us and maybe not about Matthew. What does that leave?

I kiss Gabriel and he beams at me and waves his hands and kicks his feet so I pick him up and hug him close. So far this trip has been useful if only to let me know that I like babies. Or maybe just this one. I don't want to put him down but I do and he turns his attention to the wooden seagull that flaps over his high chair. As we leave I don't dare look back in case he is waving his hands and feet at me.

I'm outside dragging my bag to the car when I feel a feather-light tap on my calf. It's Honey nudging me with her nose. Her eyes are lowered.

I glance at Gil but Suzanne is too quick for us. Take her

along, she says. Please. It's not fair to leave her here on her own all day. And I can't stand it, frankly. She's his dog. If you do find him, at least she'll be overjoyed.

I'll ride in the back with her, I tell Gil, just till she gets used to us.

Sit in front, Suzanne says with surprising force. She'll be fine on her own.

Gil looks like a man trapped in a revolving door.

But what about motels, he asks, will they allow dogs?

Just a minute, calls Suzanne, who has already dashed back into the house. When she returns, it's with a slim paperback called *Driving With Dogs*, and there are pages and pages of dog-friendly motels.

Gil is stuck and I am overjoyed. Suzanne disappears once more and reappears with a brown leather lead, a bed, a bag of dry dog food and two bowls. I feel a sudden pang of empathy for Matthew. It's hard to imagine that Suzanne doesn't always get her own way.

I stand by the front of the car while Honey sniffs the open door and the inside, and only then steps up carefully into the back. She drops her hindquarters into a graceful sit, waiting quietly.

He took her everywhere, says Suzanne, her voice sharp as glass. I avoid looking at Gil, but I can feel the expression on his face. Like me, he has begun to side with Matthew against Suzanne, if such a side exists.

Suzanne looks everywhere but at us. She runs one hand over a scrape in the front bumper. I hope you're not as bad a driver as your friend, she says.

All three of us are thinking of Owen and pretending we're

not, but the truth is that Gil is not the world's best driver. Suzanne would have a nervous breakdown if she saw the state of our London car.

We wave goodbye. Suzanne holds Gabriel's hand and makes him wave back, but she looks as if she's forgotten us already.

It's only a few miles to the motorway and though Gil seems a little hesitant at first, he relaxes once we're driving in straight lines. There are two lanes in each direction, and for a while the road is lined with fast-food joints and shops with names like Garden Furniture World and Christmas Pavilion.

Honey has the resigned air of a seasoned traveller. She seems happier in the car than in the house, though it's hard to imagine she guesses our mission. I would like to sit in the back with her. I have always wanted a dog.

Jet lag makes me hungry at funny times and I didn't eat much breakfast so now I'm starving, and when I see a sign for DINAH'S DINER NEXT RIGHT, I make Gil risk our lives to swerve across the outside lane for the slip road but it's worth it for the most beautiful silver and glass diner with metallic blue trim. Gil parks and I open the windows partway and tell Honey we'll be back. She lays her head on her paws and doesn't look at me.

Inside, the man at the till waves at us to take any booth and then brings us menus in huge padded red leatherette folders. It's translation time.

I could have Three Eggs Any Style, pancakes, hash browns, bacon, sausage patty or corned beef hash, and toast (white-wholewheat-rye-sourdough), eggs over easy, hard or sunnyside up, coffee *regular*. Regular what?

I go for two eggs sunnyside up with toast (rye), plus fresh-squeezed orange juice and at the last minute add pancakes out of greed. Gil orders the bottomless cup of coffee and French toast, which seems to come only seconds after we've ordered – big thick slices of bread all browned in egg and butter and served with icing sugar round the edges and a glass jug of maple syrup. I look at his plate and wish I'd ordered that.

Our waitress has a brown and white uniform with a green plastic badge that says her name is Merilynne. She's nice and friendly and asks where us folks are from. I just love your accent, she says to me, and then tells us she has folks on her father's side living in Lincolnshire (Lincoln-shy-er), England, who she keeps on meaning to look up and maybe drop in on someday?

I wonder if she thinks Lincolnshire is somehow connected to Abraham Lincoln, and therefore partly American.

Merilynne looks tired to me, and when she comes back carrying a tray, I'm pretty sure I know why.

This might be the largest meal I've ever eaten. I can't possibly finish the enormous pancakes, so I ask if we can take the leftovers with us, explaining that we have a dog. Makes no difference to me, says Merilynne, but not in a mean way.

Gil pays and as we go back to our car, we see Merilynne outside the diner, sitting on a step smoking a cigarette. I wonder if she'd smoke if she knew she was pregnant. I guess she'll find out soon enough.

We set off again up the highway towards Canada.

In the car, I sit in the back and open the doggy bag for Honey and find that Merilynne didn't just empty the French toast and pancake leftovers into a bag, but instead packed four pieces of bacon with about a cup of corned beef hash. *For your dog*, says a handwritten note with a smiley face after it, and it's signed *Your server Merilynne*.

Honey sniffs the bag. There are far more clues in the world for her than for any human; her sense of smell is hundreds of times keener than mine and paints whole pictures of places she hasn't been. I nibble the end of a piece of bacon and give her the rest, then put the aluminium tray on the seat of the car and she wolfs it all down in seconds. She's a tidy dog, clearing up crumbs with her neat pink tongue before settling down beside me with a sigh.

My job (other than map reading) is the radio. I lean forward between the two front seats and press the scan button to find something we both want to listen to. Mostly I can find one song we like in a row and that's it. Then there's news. Something about Washington. Something about a church scandal. Nothing about a middle-aged man who ran away from home for no reason in the middle of the day with a class to teach on the English Civil War, leaving his dog and baby and wife without even a note or a forwarding address. After a while I reach through the seats and turn it off. The feeling of trying to tune the radio matches the feeling of trying to tune in to what's happened to Matthew. No matter how much the scanner scans a few millimetres this way or that, the story won't come into focus.

The road here isn't at all like England. Most of the time it has trees on both sides, dense as a fairytale forest and seeming to go on forever. You think you're in a kind of wilderness and then suddenly the road flattens out and becomes a town, and all around are big square buildings called MAXVALUE and SUPERTREAD and WORLD OF RIBS. We are passing through one of these stretches when Gil pulls off the road in front of PHONE UNIVERSE.

We'll get you a cheap pay-as-you-go, he says, so you don't have to phone Mum by way of London.

What about you?

I've got my laptop, he says, and I smile. My father hates phones.

I'm feeling homesick. I look at Honey and bury my head in the loose folds of fur at her neck and try to love her enough to make up for what she has lost. She responds politely, gazing at me without any particular warmth.

I take her out for a walk, then put her back in the car and join Gil, who is staring at a phone that's hopelessly wrong while the girl behind the counter recites all the reasons he should buy it. Spotting the simplest and cheapest phone, I say, We'll have this one. The girl looks about seventeen. She's chewing gum, wears too much make-up and is annoyed that I have chosen such a rubbish phone when she was recommending the newest most expensive thing. All our texts are free, but not to England or Holland. The girl looks it up in a book and it turns out they're not insanely expensive, unless you go crazy and start sending texts to everyone you've ever met.

We set off again. I'm putting Suzanne and Matthew's numbers into the phone and following our progress on the map. Now that there's just one lane in each direction it's fairly slow. Mostly because of Gil's driving, which is not exactly expert and also a little bit wandery. He doesn't notice the cars piling up behind us, looking more and more annoyed. Whenever there's a straight stretch of road and the broken passing line appears, cars pull out and flash past at twice our speed. Gil doesn't look, just drives with his eyes straight ahead, his shoulders hunched over the wheel. He has to concentrate very hard because driving is not one of his natural skills. I've turned off the satnav because it jabbers constantly and annoys us both.

From the back of the map where Suzanne wrote it, the Automobile Association of America number gets added to my numbers, so that makes three people to text in America. For an instant I consider sending the AAA a text reassuring them that we're doing just fine and they don't have to worry about coming to tow us out of a ditch at the side of the road.

What I do is send Matthew a text.

Hi Matthew. It's Mila. Gil's daughter from London. We're in America looking for you. Honey's with us. She's missing you. Please tell us where you are.

I wonder if saying that Honey misses him is horrible, suggesting that none of us cares about him as much as she does. But in the end I send it, thinking he should know the truth. Then I wait. But there's no reply.

Gil and I talk a little bit about what we see, but mostly we drive in silence.

Where shall we stop for lunch? Gil asks eventually. Food becomes a big subject when you're driving.

Let's keep going till we see a restaurant we like.

So we do. We drive through a village full of big Victorian houses. Some of them look all newly painted and some look incredibly run-down. Occasionally we pass a shack that could be right out of a cartoon – windows all different sizes like someone's found them in skips, walls held together with bits of nailed wood and gaffer tape, an ancient rusted car with no wheels up on bricks, broken toys and a scraggy dog by the front porch.

This area was popular as a summer resort for rich people at the turn of the century, says Gil. Nowadays it's full of hippies and drop-outs – and probably survivalists and other scary types, he says, as we pass a tattoo parlour set in the grounds of one of the big Victorian houses.

I squint at him. Since when are you an expert?

He reaches into the side pocket of the door, hands me a fat guidebook (*Frommer's New York State*), and says, Do you think Suzanne would send us off without reference books?

I leaf through it for a minute and then go back to watching the road. How about there, I say, pointing at a white wooden house with green shutters and a wide porch. It has a hand-painted sign that says LENA'S CURIOSITIES AND CAFÉ.

At the same pace that he drives, Gil pulls off the road and glides to a stop.

The menu is nailed to a post on the big wide porch. 'Try some soup and sandwiches on Lena's homemade bread' reads the line across the top. But it's the curiosities that I'm curious about. And when we push through the door, it's clear that they're the main act.

All over the walls are stuffed heads, about fifty of them. There's a large carved eagle painted black, a stuffed fish, an etching of a herd of buffalo, an entire snake skeleton in a glass display box and a faded Japanese kimono hung on the wall. There's a big turtle shell made into a bowl and a fish tank full of crab shells. Also a pair of wooden skis with leather bindings nailed to the wall and beside them some snowshoes. They look very old. A painting in a big gold frame of an Indian squaw kneeling by a fire needs dusting. There are candles in wine bottles on every table. A pigeon I think might be stuffed turns out to be real. Behind the till is a weasel with a rat in its mouth. It's missing one glass eye. Not everyone would want to eat in these surroundings.

Can our dog come in?

It's against the law, says the woman, but she looks at Honey and nods. As long as she's quiet and doesn't mind cats.

Well, she's quiet, obviously, but I don't know what she thinks of cats. Not much, it seems, because she ignores the big grey one staring at us from her perch on the window sill and lies down under the table. For a big dog, she's good at slipping into a small space.

You folks from England? the woman asks, and Gil says, Yes.

I like your accent, she says, looking at me, and I don't know whether to say thank you.

We order bacon-lettuce-and-tomato sandwiches. I ask for root beer because I've never tried it. The person we guess is Lena brings Gil coffee without him asking. When he looks surprised, she frowns.

You don't want it?

No, he says, flustered, I mean, yes. I do.

So, what's the problem? Her face is stern.

Gil accepts the coffee.

You staying in Saratoga Springs? Racing fans?

Not really, I tell her. Not at all, in fact.

Well, that's good cos it's the wrong season, she says. You're either much too late or much too early. I went there once with my husband. Long time ago. She cackles a little and then goes off to the kitchen and comes out again with our sandwiches and sits herself down in a big comfortable chair by the door, adding up till receipts while we eat. She's a genuine one-man band, is Lena.

When we come up to pay, she and Gil chat about racing. It's a short chat. As far as I know, the sum total of Gil's knowledge about racing is Red Rum and maybe Frankie Dettori, the jockey who dismounts by leaping up in the air.

Where'd you say you folks are off to? asks Lena when the conversation fades. Gil tells her the name of the town that's closest to Matthew's cabin and she says, Still a long way to go.

And I think, You can say that again.

14

Have you ever seen a terrier at work? It stands stock-still, quivering all over with anticipation, waiting for the moment the slip collar comes off. Then there's a fraction of a second where it seems to explode, launching itself forward at its prey. And a terrible snarling and growling and shaking and squeaking as it gets to grips, quite literally, with the rat. It's not nice, but it is impressive. And quick.

It is not a sense of responsibility or a desire to please that makes a dog do this. It's what they're bred to do. They can't help it. If I were a dog, I'd be part terrier.

The rational part of me makes a flow chart with two columns, headed MATTHEW IS DEAD and MATTHEW IS ALIVE.

If Matthew is dead, there are four possibilities:

(A) Murder
(B) Suicide
(C) Accidental death
(D) Illness – stroke or heart attack

At Suzanne's, I Googled cases of people who suddenly walk away from their homes and families. Some of the reasons are:

(A) Madness
(B) Amnesia
(C) Money problems
(D) Marital woes
(E) Secret second family
(F) Depression
(G) Fired from job but hasn't told wife
(H) Crisis of religious faith or near-death experience
(I) Terrible secret
(J) Kidnapping
(K) Mental illness
(L) Doesn't know why

Many of these reasons are confusing. Why wouldn't you tell your wife if you lost your job? What's so bad about a crisis of faith? What sort of secret? Someday I'll understand more of these things. At the moment I just have to think them through. Not everything you want to know is explained properly on Google.

To be thorough, I have to take into account the possibility that Matthew was kidnapped. But why would someone kidnap a middle-aged professor of British history? I have no idea. For all I know he has links to the Chinese underworld, about which I know less than nothing, except what I once saw in a TV movie.

Despite the fact that I can sweep a crime scene for rats like a terrier, I frequently have trouble putting clues together due to gaps in my knowledge of the world. I could do with a middle-aged accomplice. Gil is not the person for this job. Miss Marple would be better.

Take marriage. Marieka and Gil have been together for twenty years but have never married. Marieka says it's because where she grew up, women were independent and didn't want to have some man put a ring on their finger and tell them to do the washing-up.

This makes me laugh. I can't imagine either of my parents acting like that. When I asked Gil why he and Marieka never married, he said, I wouldn't dream of presuming.

Presuming what? I asked.

I don't remember if he answered.

Matthew had lots of girlfriends but didn't get married till he met Suzanne. He was forty-two. This tells me something too, but I'm not sure what. Whenever I imagine him, it's on a mountain with a frozen beard. Not the sort of person you imagine getting married.

Most of my friends at school have parents who look like married people are supposed to look – women in dresses, men in ties. Catlin's mum trained as a teacher but stays home each day while Catlin's dad goes to work for a software company. Every time I see her, I think she looks out of place in her house as if she doesn't know where to sit.

Gil glances away from the road for the briefest of seconds and asks what I'm doing and I tell him I'm thinking as hard as I can, in circles and retrogrades and whatever else I can drum up. I ask him the same question and he says he's driving Matthew's wife's car up towards Canada. I know that, I answer. But what else?

I'm thinking too, he says. I'm thinking about my fool of a friend.

What have you concluded? I ask, ignoring the comment about the fool.

Nothing, Gil says. What about you?

I'm trying to be methodical, I say – slightly pointedly, because he never is. I'm trying to organize the possibilities. Once we've done that, it will make our job a little easier.

Oh, you think so?

Yes, I do. I look over at him. He's facing forward because he's driving, but he swivels an eye on me.

Look, I say. You can't just let your thoughts float around in the ether and hope eventually they'll connect with something. It's absurd.

No it's not, Gil says. Lots of good things happen that way. Penicillin. Teflon. Smart dust. Something happens that you weren't expecting and it shifts the outcome completely. You have to be open to it.

When I open my brain, I tell him, things bounce around and fall out. They don't connect with anything. Maybe I haven't got enough points of reference stored up yet.

You're young, he says, that's probably it. When I let *my* thoughts float around, I trust that they'll latch on to something useful in the end or make an association I wouldn't necessarily have predicted. I'm trusting that they'll find the right thought to complete, all by themselves. The right bit of fact to go *ping*. You have to trust your brain sometimes.

Maybe, I'm thinking. But so far I only trust my brain up

to a point. Without guidance it could skew off in any crazy direction or just wander into a cul de sac for a snooze. That's why I make charts. Anyway, I say to Gil, I hope it happens. I really do. Because my flow chart hasn't got me anywhere useful.

Gil smiles without taking his eyes off the road. We'll get there.

You think so? Privately I'm feeling doubtful, but I don't say so.

Yes. One way or another, we will.

OK, I say, and then I stop making a flow chart, reach back and pat Honey, who's dozing, and look out of the window for a while. But it's hard to stop my brain from thinking.

Tell me everything you know about the accident, I say to Gil.

Which accident?

The one that killed Owen.

He glances at me. Is that relevant?

Of course it's relevant. How can I understand Matthew without all the facts? You never know which ones will turn out to be important.

OK, Gil says. OK. But I'm not sure I remember everything.

I sit very still and wait.

So. Matt picked Owen up after a swimming practice, says Gil. It was evening. Winter. Dark. They had to take the highway for a short distance, just long enough for one of those big articulated lorries to skid and crash into the back of their car. It was crushed.

The whole car?

The back of the car.

And what about Matthew?

He was uninjured. Bruised a bit.

Wait . . . Owen was sitting in the back?

Yes.

That's strange.

I don't know, Perguntador. Maybe American kids have to sit in the back, because it's safer or something.

Little kids. He was taller than Suzanne.

Maybe they'd just dropped someone off or he wanted to stretch out. Maybe there was shopping in the front. Sports kit.

Maybe. And then?

They were in the fast lane. An ambulance came. Police. I remember Suzanne telling Marieka at the time that Matthew was completely exonerated by the police.

Exonerated? I'm frowning, confused.

Found not guilty.

Not guilty of what? Was he a suspect?

I don't think so. It's just normal, I guess. Make sure he didn't fall asleep at the wheel or was on drugs or anything.

I think about this. Exonerated? The grieving father? I try to picture the scene. Once more I look at Gil. What about the lorry? I ask.

It was coming up behind them. The driver tried to swerve and flipped over the centre strip. The back of the lorry must have swung round and smashed Matt's car.

And the lorry driver?

I guess he died too.

You *guess* he died?

He died.

A moving picture takes shape in my brain. Matthew and Owen in the fast lane, far left. The lorry coming up behind them. Not in the same lane, presumably, not in the fast lane. One lane to the right. What causes a huge lorry to skid?

Are you sure he tried to swerve, or are you just making that up?

Gil thinks. Pretty sure. Most of my information came from Marieka, he says. I never had the heart to ask for more details. Why?

Well, if you're going to crash into someone, especially when you're coming up from behind, you don't skid first. Do you?

Maybe it was icy. Maybe he was pulling over into Matt's lane and didn't see him.

Those guys drive for a living. Would they make a mistake like that? And how often have you seen one of those huge lorries in the fast lane? And even if he *did* pull into Matthew's lane, the lorry driver would have been fine. Matt would have spun and crashed, not the truck. Can't you see it in your head?

Despite a thorough understanding of my father's limitations, I feel impatient.

Not really, he says. What about ice?

Maybe.

Or maybe he was tired.

Tired or not, I can't see how it was the lorry driver's fault. The picture in my head is clear now. I can see Matthew's car brake or drift out of lane or do something that causes the lorry behind him to brake so hard, he skids and flips over the central reservation, crushing the back of Matthew's car with the fishtail. If Owen had been sitting in the front, he'd have survived.

Strictly speaking, there's nothing so strange about sitting in the back seat of a car when it's just you and your father. But if you were having a fight, would you sit in the back? Wouldn't you just hunch in the corner of the front seat staring out of the window, feeling wronged? And if you were tired, wouldn't you also just slouch down in the front? Maybe Owen liked sitting in the back, or he'd hurt his leg in practice and wanted to stretch out, or there was a big bag of shopping in the front seat.

I store the question in a file in my head marked M for maybe.

15

The sign reads SCENIC DRIVE and points off to the right. Gil turns. I guess we may as well enjoy the view, he says, having come this far.

I thought we were on a mission. Life and death.

We are, Gil says. But Suzanne said it's really beautiful.

Am I imagining things or is everyone treating this trip like some kind of half-hearted holiday thing, like a treasure hunt to keep us occupied as long as we just happen to be in America anyway?

I look at Gil. Seriously? The scenic route?

He looks back. Would you rather stick to the motorway?

OK. OK. I check the map. There appears to be a big long lake coming up on the right and lo and behold, the dense trees all at once give way to long views across a narrow bright-blue stretch of water with mountains beyond.

Look! I say, and then regret it as Gil slows even more and in the mirror I can see the driver behind us, fuming. On the next clear stretch the guy passes us with a huge roar of his engine. From the cab of his insanely large pick-up, he shoots us a contemptuous look. There are guns on a rack in the back seat. *Guns?*

Did you see that?

Gil nods. They must be for decoration, he says. Hunting season's October.

I stare at him. Did you memorize the guidebook or what?

You can't shoot animals who've just given birth or are pregnant. Even in America. So, it's autumn for slaughter, just like at home.

Great. Now I'm scanning the edges of the woods for bears and deer with offspring. Doomed, yes. But not right away.

A couple of miles later, the view breaks off and we're driving through a pretty little town balanced on the edge of the lake and the sun makes hard reflections on the water. We drive past a boat-builder and a couple of big elegant old Victorian houses. Gil pulls in at an ice-cream place.

Without asking, he orders tall spirals of ice creams for us both, vanilla and chocolate mixed, and a cup of coffee for himself. We sit outside at a wooden picnic table. The air is cool and the sun warm enough to induce sleep. Neither of us feels any rush to get back on the road.

Gil picks up a local paper that someone's left behind and he's reading it back to front, studying the classifieds. I break the bottom off my cone and feed it to Honey and then she and I head down to the water with my ice cream dripping down my hand. I sit on the grass and stare at the lake and the mountains with the sun on the back of my neck. Honey's beside me. I give her my ice cream to finish. According to Gil, Red Indians once lived here. You can see why they chose it.

We circle back to Gil. Look, he says, we could buy an above-ground swimming pool for just four hundred bucks. Or a Nearly New Weed-Whacker. He flips pages and I look over his shoulder at a picture of a raccoon family caught on someone's CCTV. They look furtive, like raccoon criminals.

Honey positions herself in the sun and lowers herself down, head across her paws. She is a beautiful creature with a noble head, but I can see that under her thick white coat her body is gaunt. She is old. About twelve, Gil thinks. My age.

Ninety miles to go. On these roads that's at least two hours, he says, and I suddenly wish we were making this journey for pleasure. I would prefer to be meandering at no pace at all, stopping and going just on the whim of the moment. But even the scenic route can't stop me thinking about Matthew and the pieces missing from the jigsaw. Most of the pieces. All I've got so far is sky.

Think, I think. Think of the facts: Owen died three years ago. In a collision with a lorry. It wasn't Matthew's fault. He was completely exonerated by the police.

When you're looking for answers, it's the things that nag at your brain that count.

Exonerated?

Gil flips over to the front page, where there's a large picture of the winners of the local ten-mile Fun Run. It's mostly women with their arms around each other, grinning. At the bottom there's a notice about hunting licences and a list of regulations, with a big jolly headline that says HUNTING SEASON'S COMING SOON.

I read more. The notice says you must be over the age of twelve to apply for a licence, and a ten-hour safety course is required for new applicants. It also says that 189,000 deer were shot last year in New York State with only twenty-nine injuries to humans, none fatal. One hundred and eighty-nine thousand deer. And three hundred and eighteen bears. Who would want to kill a bear? You can't even eat them. The thought of all those dead animals depresses me. A picture that goes with the article shows a happy guy holding up the lolling head of a dead deer. The caption says '*Steve Wilson and a nice ten-pointer*'.

What sort of place is this?

We flop back into the car. It's hot, and once we get going I turn the air conditioning on. Honey pants a little in the back. We've lingered and dawdled and it's late afternoon before we finally leave the highway for a smaller road. Gil stops for petrol. He pays and returns to the car, but instead of driving off, he sits back, hands resting on the steering wheel, and turns to me.

What should we do now? he asks. We can get there tonight if we drive straight through.

Let's not, I say.

It may just be nerves but I don't like the idea of confronting anything in the half-dark, whether it's Matthew or not-Matthew. Plus, I don't want our journey to be over so soon. What if we find Matthew and he's furious that we've chased him all the way up to the Canadian border after he and Suzanne had a fight and decided to be apart for a while? Or what if we find him with a new girlfriend? Or some kind of contraband? Twenty-eight kilos of cocaine. What if he hates us for coming all this way after him like he's some sort of criminal? What if he *is* some sort of criminal?

I don't say all this, but Gil nods anyway. Maybe he's thinking the same thing.

OK.

I'm staring at the map. We could go to Lake Placid. It looks quite big on the map. What's there?

The 1980 Winter Olympics, Gil says, and passes me the guidebook. Have a look.

I read the entry, which reports that Lake Placid is a charming town with a delightful mix of restaurants, retail facilities (retail *facilities*?), antique shops and sporting goods outlets. '*You'll find something for everyone in Lake Placid!*' says the book in a grammatically annoying way, and with all that stuff going on and all those retail facilities I'm finding it hard to imagine that Lake Placid is actually very placid.

I read some more and then look at Gil. Could we stay there tonight?

They'll have plenty of motels, anyway, he says, and pulls off the road to look at the map. Over his shoulder I see a picture of the ski jump built for the old Olympics.

Christ, it's terrifying, he says, following the direction of my gaze. It's hard to imagine anyone actually skiing down that thing.

I close my eyes for a few seconds and think what it would feel like to drop on to that near-vertical slope, fly down in the crouch position, then explode off the lip of the jump at two hundred miles an hour. I would land on the ice with a splat like a blood pie.

Half an hour later, we pass the real thing. We pull over and get out to look at it. Gil stares. Never in a million years, he says, and sounds like he means it. But at least it has a lift to the top. Not like a mountain. What about you?

74

Me? I shake my head. No way. Do you miss those days? I ask, thinking of mountain climbing.

Gil shakes his head. No.

Why did you do it?

I don't know, Mila. I was young. And Matt was so convincing. If he said climbing was the thing, we climbed.

God knows where they'd have ended up if they'd lived in different times. I'm imagining my father and Matt as highwaymen or in the French resistance, taking terrible risks. As Hitler Youth.

Would Matthew ski down that?

Gil smiles. He'd probably try.

Didn't you like climbing at all?

I don't know, Gil says. Of course I did. I don't think I'd have started on my own, but I got addicted to the kick.

Adrenalin, I suggest, and he nods.

We climb back into the car, drive into town and park. It's pretty and well-tended, and though I've never been to Switzerland, it looks like my idea of Switzerland – quaint little wooden shops and restaurants facing the lake with the mountains beyond. Minus the guys in lederhosen. And the mountains aren't very big, not like the Alps.

While Gil looks for a real newspaper, I try texting again.

Matthew. It's Gil's daughter Mila again. We need to find you. Pls txt me when you get this message.

After some consideration, I take out the line about needing to find him. And the Gil's daughter bit too. The world is not filled with people called Mila.

Matthew. It's Mila. Txt me when you get this.

I wait for some time but there's no reply so I text Marieka just to say hi and then Catlin. Neither of them answers either.

We shop around town for a while, looking at things in windows. There's an old wooden sleigh in the antique shop with some blue-and-white jugs, and a bookshop with a beautiful view of the lake.

And then, in the window of the deli, I find the Easter egg of my dreams. The pattern on it is cowboys – cowboys with lassos, cowboys riding cow ponies and bucking broncos, cowboys herding cows, cowboys with cowgirls. It's such an incongruous theme for an Easter egg that I burst out laughing. And to top it off, it's enormous.

Oh my god, it's perfect! Catlin will die of happiness, I say, and Gil rolls his eyes, no doubt thinking of the price.

But when we go in and ask how much it is, the deli man says it's not for sale.

I can't sell it in all good faith, he says. It's left over from two years ago so it'll be stale. Lots of people have asked to buy it, but I'm afraid it's staying right here. Hi ho, Silver!

I can understand his point but I want this egg so badly I'm running a whole series of silent scenarios that include breaking into his shop in the dead of night and stealing it.

I don't suppose there's another one?

He shakes his head.

Does it bring in more business for the other eggs? I ask, determined to blind him with the logic of getting rid of it.

He shakes his head again, mournfully this time. I have no

idea. It's kind of a folly, he says. But it looks good in the window, don't you think? Lured you in, anyway.

The other salesperson laughs.

See? he says. They all laugh at me. But everyone loves my cowboy egg. Hi ho, Silver!

I'm wondering what's with the Hi ho, Silver, but what I say is, Please could you at least consider selling it? I have a friend at home whose parents are getting divorced and she's really upset and depressed and this egg would definitely cheer her up. I sneak a peek at him to see if my story is working. She's desperate, I say in my saddest, lowest voice.

Well, he says slowly, shaking his head. That's a pretty sad story. But I'm afraid it's out of the question. It's not for sale. And besides, it's two years old. It won't even taste good.

I think of Catlin. She wouldn't care what it tasted like. It's something else she wants, from me. A sign. This egg is a great big blinking sign that says, We are friends forever and we laugh at the same things.

You'd be asking me to disappoint a whole town, says the child-hating deli guy. Maybe next year.

I know it's only an egg but I feel like crying. Maybe another amazing egg will appear somewhere on our journey. Maybe America is full of them. But in my heart I know it isn't. And then I try to convince myself that the perfect Easter egg doesn't matter, especially when Matthew might be dead, and how on earth would I have managed to get it home anyway? But the egg would matter to Catlin. I know it would. It would make her happy, even just for a minute.

Dad buys a bottle of local organic hand-squeezed artisan

apple juice and I glare at him because I hate the idea of giving this man any of our money.

A collar of reindeer bells on the door rings as we go out. Hi ho, Silver! the man calls, but I don't look back.

16

It's starting to get dark so we park at one of the motels, and the receptionist tells us they're full because of Easter vacation. Try the Mountain View Motor Inn, she says, it's a half-mile down the road.

We get back in the car and because the road is so curly, it seems a long way till we find it. But there's a little dog symbol next to the credit-card stickers on the office window, so we're in luck. I tell the guy behind the desk that my dad is parking the car and he says he likes my accent, am I Australian? When Gil comes in he offers us a family room for no more than a regular double.

So now I have my own room attached to his with my own TV. I like this. Private but connected. There's a snug corner in my bit that's perfect for Honey's bed and she curls up there like it's where she's always lived.

She doesn't need much exercise at her age, Gil says, and I think how strange it is that at twelve she's old and I'm young. He takes her out anyway and I text Catlin.

No sign of our missing guy I write.

Boo bloody hoo comes the text in return, and I'm shocked and upset because I thought we were friends again. But the phone bleeps a second later.

Dad's moved out. Mum cries all day.

Oh. I've known Catlin long enough and can hear her voice, small and furious.

Oh Cat, I text back, **I'm REALLY sorry xxxxxxx**

It takes a while for the next one but I know what it's going to say before it arrives.

I don't give a shit.

Which is more or less definite proof that she does.

Love you loads I text back, but she doesn't answer.

Gil returns with Honey. Temperature's dropping, he says, then gives her one of the dog chews Suzanne packed and pours some dinner for her out of the box. She sniffs it and turns away. No left-over bacon, no French toast, no ice cream, no deal.

We leave Honey and walk next door to a big square restaurant done up to look like a cartoon version of Thailand with huge carved pillars and a pointy roof painted all over red and gold. My Thai, it's called, and it's nearly empty. The waitress says to sit anywhere and we do, and then when she comes over again we order Pad Thai and green curry and she says she likes my accent which I never know quite how to answer. I get up to look at the big orange fish in the tank near the till while we wait for the food to come. I'm really hoping that any fish in our meal don't come from that tank.

The food arrives and it's not too bad, though the Pad Thai is quite sticky. Gil orders a Thai beer, drinks it and asks for another.

What will we do if we find Matthew at the cabin? I ask.

I guess we'll talk to him, Gil says.

What will we do if we don't find him?

Gil shrugs. One step at a time. At least we'll have had a genuine American experience on the way, eh, Perguntador?

As we eat, the restaurant fills up and I can't help gathering facts about the people who eat here. Tourists, mainly. Some speak a weird-sounding French, which Gil says is French-Canadian. The American families don't talk to each other much, though some of them shout at their children. One father I catch saying grace before they start to eat while his teenage son looks around, mortified. One man knows the waitress. He's either related to her or a friend or he comes here a lot. A few people don't bother with the menu. They know what they want. Two boys come in and when they order beers the waitress asks for ID, which they don't have. But she's nice, acts like it's no big deal and brings them Cokes instead. People order huge plates of food and if there's anything left over, they ask for doggy bags. I wouldn't give this food to Honey; it's not healthy.

At last we go back to our hotel room and I watch TV with the sound turned off while Gil reads, but it's mostly ads for losing weight or gigantic pizzas. As usual I don't remember falling asleep but wake up in the middle of the night with the TV off and the neon glow of the motel sign seeping in through the blinds. In Gil's room, the reading light is still on.

A girl at school told everyone the story of a murderer who hid the body of a dead woman inside the box mattress in a motel. For ten days, people slept in the bed and the body wasn't discovered until the hotel investigated complaints about a foul smell in the room.

The idea of all those people sleeping on top of a dead woman scared me so much that I didn't sleep for a week. The girl knew it would have that effect. You'd have to be either super- or sub-human to get that picture out of your head.

This is something I've considered before: the story that ends up in your head unasked-for, or that gets deposited by someone like that girl. I have a file of horrible images, but I won't share them with you. What if I stuck one here, in the middle of a paragraph you happen to be reading, like a landmine? You'd never be able to forget it; it would be part of you forever, like a bit of shrapnel in your brain. It's bad enough I told the one about the body in the mattress.

I feel lonely all of a sudden for Marieka.

Hi Mum. We're hot on the trail but is it the right one? I don't think we're very good detectives. Defectives more like. Haha. How are u? Miss u tons. Love Mila

Gil looks up from his book and asks why I'm still awake. I shrug, and get a text back.

What are you doing up at this hour? Bet you and Dad are great detectives. I love you. XOXO Mum

This makes me feel better. I get up and climb into bed with Gil for a while and he puts his book away so we can watch a nature programme on fish who live in the abyss, the deepest part of the ocean. Dad's got his arm around me. Being in such a strange room with only the television for light makes me feel sad and lost in a deep place like the abyss. I push my nose up against Gil's shirt and close my eyes and can smell home, which makes me feel better.

I know Gil wishes I would read more but I prefer watching TV, preferably with the sound turned off. Just the pictures. If there's a crime drama on, it's obvious whodunnit from practically the first frame; particularly with no sound. The minute an actor knows he's the bad guy, you can see it in his face, the way he walks. If I were a director I wouldn't tell the cast whodunnit till the very last minute.

I heard of a famous detective writer who never knew who the murderer was in his books till he got to the end. Personally, I wouldn't leave such an important decision to a bunch of invented characters.

After a while I go back to my own room and drag Honey's bed up to my end. She stands while I do it, then pads over and lies down so I can reach out and pat her. I close my eyes but, no matter what I do, the possibility of a dead body stuffed through a slit in the mattress haunts me like an evil smell in the air. I text Matthew.

Don't you care about making everyone worry? Txt back when you get this.

I don't bother signing it.

Gil is still awake. Gil, I whisper loudly.

Hmmm? he answers.

Let's call Marieka.

It's not even seven a.m. in Holland.

I'd forgotten about the time difference. She was awake a while ago, I tell him. My voice sounds small, even to me.

We don't have much credit on the phone, Gil says, but he nods. Marieka picks up on the first ring.

Are you OK? She says she'll phone back, and does. Why are you still awake? She sounds concerned. Where's Gil?

He's right here, I say. I'm sorry to call. I couldn't help it.

It's fine, sweetheart. Where are you?

We're at a motel. Near Lake Placid. We're going to Matthew's cabin tomorrow. Today.

I guess nobody's heard anything from him, she says, but doesn't wait for an answer. She knows that any hearing from him would have been the first thing reported. How are you, my darling? Are you lonely?

A little, I say. Though at this moment it would be more honest to say a lot.

Well, she says, I guess you'll either find him or you won't.

That narrows it down. I laugh. Her voice reassures me. How are your concerts going?

Just rehearsals, she says. First one's tomorrow. No surprises so far. How's your father? Why can't you sleep?

Dad's fine, I say. But we miss you. Do you want to talk to

him? I pass the phone over and Gil blinks. Without his glasses he looks like a slightly different person.

We'll just take it as it comes, he says after a minute. And then, Of course, with a serious expression. Though she's perfectly capable of taking care of herself. Another pause. I know. I'll try to remember that. He throws me a kiss. That's from Marieka, he says to me, and then to her, I love you too, my darling. Play well. And hangs up.

He looks at me critically. Your mum says you're only young and need your sleep.

You're only middle-aged and need your sleep too.

Good point, he says. And then, OK. We'll both go to sleep. We'll need our wits about us tomorrow.

I say goodnight to Gil and go back to my own bed but too many questions are keeping me awake. I send another text from under the covers.

Matthew where are you?

I don't expect an answer so am not surprised when one doesn't come.

Sometime later, the bleep of the phone wakes me from a deep sleep.

I'm nowhere says the message.

It's from Matthew.

17

Gil once told me about a play in which a man falls in love with a goat.

I laughed. In *love*, in love? And he nodded.

But surely . . . not in *that way*, I said, and he smiled and nodded again. *There's nowt so queer as folk.*

And I remember thinking: that's for damned sure.

When I told her, Catlin said, Well, that's just plain sick, unless it was one really hot goat. And then she made a face and skipped off to smoke a fag and eat horrible chicken and chips from a cardboard box with her new best friends who didn't seem to see me when we passed on the street. Or maybe they were too busy laughing at jokes only they understood.

Gil explained that the goat story is a metaphor for some uncontrollable form of passion, like being a child molester or falling in love with your sister. The mystery of the whole Matthew situation makes me wonder if he carries a secret so devastating that the world would tilt if it found out. Or is it only devastating in his head?

What did Matthew mean, *I'm nowhere*?

I am about to wake Gil and tell him that I've heard from Matthew. Gil, look, a message! He's not dead after all.

But I don't.

Then it's morning and I'm packing my suitcase while Gil shaves. And again I am about to tell Gil about the text.

But still I don't.

We will almost certainly be meeting Matthew at the cabin today. And I know the message would upset Gil.

And yet. He's the adult and I'm the child. I'm worried by the message, but feel protective of my fifty-eight-year-old father. Is it my job to shield him from the icy chill in Matthew's message?

In the blink of an eye, the world has turned upside down. Come along, I could say to him now, don't dawdle, and have you brushed your teeth?

By the time I find a grassy spot to walk Honey and Gil pays the bill, it's nearly eleven. We go back into town and find a place for breakfast on the main street. I have waffles and Gil has scrambled eggs with a large side order of sausages to replace the boring food Honey will no longer eat.

When Gil offers the foil tray of sausages, Honey swallows them down in big chomps. I open the door to the back seat and she hops in and stretches out, licking her chops. Gil and I glance at each other, a little guiltily. We are not responsible dog parents.

So far, we've been following decent-size roads, but they get smaller as we drive north, till at last we're bumping along an unpaved road through dense trees. Honey stands now, both front paws on the armrest between the front seats, her nose pointing through the windscreen, ears pricked. Has she been here before? Does she remember the road? The map shows that there's a lake nearby but we can't see it. Yellow STRICTLY NO HUNTING notices are nailed to trees along one stretch of land. There's something wild about the woods here. I hope the bears remain hidden in case some lunatic with a gun decides to ignore the signs.

Every few minutes another spindly dirt road branches off from the one we're on, sometimes marked with a name or a postbox, sometimes with a number, sometimes with nothing at all. Gil looks anxious, squinting at his map.

We're almost there, he says. It should be just at the end of this road. He turns over the paper with Suzanne's directions on it, as if looking for more information about what we might find there.

Abruptly, the road ends. It turns into a footpath through trees, not wide enough for a car.

There is no building in sight.

Come on, says Gil. This must be it.

We step out of the car.

It's a beautiful morning, much colder than yesterday. Sunshine floats down through the trees. There's a breeze, which makes the leaves rustle and the branches creak. I can hear things scurrying in the underbrush. Small things. I picture them, greyish, brownish, darting rodents with sharp bright frightened little eyes and sharp little feet, tiny and unsettled by our presence.

I squint deep into the woods, hoping to catch a glimpse

of a moose, but all I can see are more trees. The floor of the woods is covered with pine needles and fallen twigs; years of decay make the path soft underfoot. Honey stands very still, quivering a little, her nose in the air. Does she remember being here with Matthew? Does she smell him? Is he here? She's sniffing the ground now and my heart races as she takes off down the path. He must be here. He must be.

We follow.

Gil stops at a clearing. The cabin is made of wood, painted but weathered and peeling. Windows circle the little house and are all shut. The front door is painted green, shut tight, but there's an outer screen door that doesn't seem to close properly; it blows open and shut very slightly with a squeak. Honey circles the house, whining. She stops, throws back her head and howls, then resumes her running – back and forth, round and round. Distracted and slightly mad.

Presumably Honey's been here before with Matthew and remembers. She might smell his presence, or the memory of his presence. Like us, she hopes for resolution.

Gil looks agitated. Takes a deep breath. No one peers at us through the windows, no one comes to greet us. He calls hello. We approach the house and I take his hand. Honey has stopped running and stands very still, sniffing the air.

What have we here? Gil asks softly.

What we have here is a person staying at a cabin in the middle of the woods, who is either not here right now or pretending not to be here right now in the hope that we'll go away.

Look, I say to Gil.

There's a cat. And one thing I know for absolute certain is that big well-fed cats don't live alone in the woods. This cat is a stripy black-and-brown tortoiseshell, which makes her almost invisible in the shadows beside the house. She crouches perfectly still, watching us as if we're prey. Her eyes are yellowish green, and she knows I've seen her. Cats may not be the world's most intellectual creatures but they're excellent observers. This cat turns its attention from us to something in front of it. Maybe that's what she was doing before we arrived, waiting for something to come out of a hole. No sane cat would crouch all day waiting for a translator and his daughter to wander down the path looking for someone who may or may not happen to live here.

I watch the cat, watch it freeze, eyes intent on the ground, watch her swipe with her front paw, then straighten up, paw planted firmly on the ground. She stares down as if mesmerized, then sinks forward, swift as thought, coming up again with the mouse in her mouth. She tosses the mouse a little up in the air and I can actually see the tiny creature scramble, trying to regain its feet, too late. The cat has the advantage. When the mouse reconnects with earth, the cat is already batting at it with its two front paws, like a footballer dribbling a ball. I find it almost impossible to stop watching this game, despite the fact that I am not entirely certain whose side I'm on.

Gil is walking towards the cabin. He opens the screen door and knocks loudly but there is no answer. He calls out. Hello! Anybody here? Then tries the door. It's locked. He looks at me, cups his hands together and presses his face to the window. Curtains block his view.

The cat hates him, I can see it. It resents having its game

ruined by this shouting man. A moment of inattention and suddenly the cat rises up on its hind legs, looks left and right like a cartoon cat seeking a cartoon mouse, then sits and begins to lick one paw, casually, as if it couldn't care less that the best game of the day has been spoilt.

In all our nervous imaginings of the big confrontation, we hadn't really considered that someone might be here but not here. We circle the cabin but there's nothing to see. It is occupied, I know that much. It isn't just the cat. There is nothing empty or abandoned about the place – the flower beds are tidy and look as if someone might recently have been planting flowers. Metal hooks hold back heavy wooden shutters. The house seems to breathe slightly with occupation.

Gil looks in, through the door this time.

Someone's living here, he says. And as he says it I swing round to look at a little outhouse, nearly invisible in a stand of trees. I walk towards it and Gil follows. It's very basic. Beside the outhouse there's a compost pit for rubbish – a square wooden door weighed down with a large stone. I lift it and there's our evidence: egg cartons, newspapers and kitchen waste. Peelings, banana skins, bones. All recent, including the newspapers.

I concentrate and let the feelings of the little cabin seep into my head. It is a woman here, I feel that strongly. But someone else too. Could it be Matthew?

A woman lives here, I say.

How do you know? asks Gil, and I look at him because he and I have had the how-do-I-know conversation too many times in our lives.

I know because I know. Sometimes I can say, Aha! An

empty bottle of nail varnish. That's how I know. Meat in a can – no woman eats meat in a can. A dozen empty beer cans, the cheap sort, there's a hint. But usually it's nothing so obvious. I look at a picture and I see the things that aren't visible at that moment. It's not that I'm some sort of mystic; I just see a constellation of tiny facts too small for other people to notice. I don't specifically register each element of the constellation but the overall impression will be clear. The Bear. The Hunter. The Swan.

Do you know the story of Clever Hans?

Clever Hans was an Arab horse living in Germany around the turn of the last century. His owner billed him as the cleverest horse on earth. He could add, subtract, multiply, calculate square roots and tell time, and would communicate the answers to his astonished audience by tapping out numbers with his hoof. Even with his master's back turned, or different questioners, Clever Hans was uncannily accurate.

In 1907, thirteen external examiners were sent from Berlin to validate Hans's feats. And for some time they were stuck. It seemed the horse really could perform difficult mathematical calculations.

But then they began to experiment. They tried blindfolding Hans and his accuracy dropped. At last, they hit upon the idea of asking questions that the questioner himself couldn't answer. And that was it. Hans faltered, refusing even to make an attempt. What was it? Could he read minds?

It turned out that Clever Hans was picking up almost imperceptible clues from his questioner's posture that told him when to stop tapping. When Hans reached the correct answer, the questioner's heart rate might increase, his shoulders might tense slightly or relax slightly – not enough of a sign for any of the humans in the room to recognize or interpret, not so much that the questioner himself recognized what he was doing. But enough for the horse. In other words, poor Hans wasn't so clever at mathematics after all.

Merely astonishingly gifted at interpreting that which no one else could see.

Mila is a perfectly nice name and I have never been dissatisfied with it, but if my parents had happened to name me after that horse, I would have been greatly honoured.

18

If the person or persons who are living at Matthew's cabin is or are actually Matthew, then our hunt is over. If they are not Matthew, they may know where he is. Something tells me that he's not here. I can't explain the feeling. Something about Honey's howl, the way her excitement waned, a dog following an old trail.

We will have to return.

It is three quarters of an hour back to the Mountain View Motor Inn where we stop and tell them we will be staying another night. Then we head into town. We have some time to kill and Gil needs to buy a new razor.

While he decides between the blue and the silver, I ask him for five dollars to buy a small stuffed moose.

We're so far north here that you might say we're inundated with moose. There's the Mighty Moose Café in town and Moose Martin Antiques, in front of which is a huge wooden carved moose, almost as big as a real one. There are paintings of moose in the office of the Mountain View Motor Inn. The place we have breakfast, though not named after a moose, has a drawing of a moose on the menu.

I'd like to see a real moose. Given that I live in North London, I'm guessing it's now or never.

We've been here less than twenty-four hours and already everything looks familiar. It's a small town; you can walk from one end to the other in about ten minutes. It would be strange to live here for twenty years when in just a few hours it's begun to feel like home.

Though I like being with Gil and having a mission and possibly being able to make a difference by finding Matthew, I'm also fairly homesick and there's something nice about feeling that we belong here in this funny place. I fantasize about staying here forever. Marieka comes to join us and we buy one of the pretty wooden farmhouses on the road out of town, I ride a big farm horse to school every day, Catlin comes to visit in the summer, Gil works by a wood fire all winter and Marieka practises her violin in a cosy studio that used to be the dairy.

Then I turn off the fantasy because, really? I can't see any of us living here at all.

Whenever I remember, I text Cat. **No fun without you, Missing your face** or **What's the latest?** But she doesn't answer. It's hard to know with texts whether someone isn't getting your messages or doesn't like you or what. Maybe she's gone back to her cool gang and doesn't want to be my friend any more or maybe she's run out of credit and can't ask her parents for money cos they're getting divorced.

There's a whole rack of cards in the bookshop and I buy some with silk-screened pictures of loons and owls for Marieka then wander next door to Ammo Depot, which sells big padded jackets up to size XXXL in camouflage green print and bright orange, and tartan wool duck-hunting hats straight out of an Elmer Fudd cartoon (complete with flaps you can unsnap to pull down over your ears), and other stuff like leather and rubber boots, hunting knives with bone handles, canteens, tents, groundsheets and duck whistles. I love this shop. Everything in it is so foreign. There's a young guy lounging around among the tents and fishing rods, and he's about to ask if he can help me but I look away quickly, shy in front of a stranger in this shop full of things I'd have no clue what to do with.

Then he goes behind the counter, unlocks a cabinet and starts straightening up boxes of bullets, and it dawns on me that, actually, this shop is all about killing. Suddenly everything I notice is a skinning knife or a laser scope. I get freaked out and leave.

In the doorway I glance back and the boy is looking at me. At first I think he might have noticed that I'm interesting and foreign, but it's far more likely that he thinks I'm a shoplifter. Who else would run out of a shop so fast?

Next door there's a second-hand bookshop that might be full of treasures but isn't, quite. I find a book about Laura Ingalls Wilder's real life, complete with actual photographs of her parents, and I kind of wish I hadn't because I love her books and the photos of Laura Ingalls Wilder's real-life parents make them look like religious fundamentalists. The drawings of Pa with his beard playing the fiddle made him seem cheerful and warm, but the man in the photos looks cold and distant. And weird. Ma, who was beautiful and kind in the books, here just looks sour. Gil says that in the early days of photography it wasn't considered proper to smile at the camera.

A few minutes later I find him at the other side of the shop staring at a book.

Look at this, he says. It's old and a bit damp, with brown spots on the pages, but he's so excited that I'm excited too. He opens the cover to look for a price. The mark in pencil says $3.

What on earth is this doing here? he asks, showing me the title. It's an old translation of the book he's working on now. What a strange coincidence, he says. Not exactly the sort of book you'd find just anywhere.

It's the town, I think, welcoming us with little gifts.

When I was eight I found a violin in a skip that turned out to be worth £9,000. I just caught a glimpse of it out of the corner of my eye as I walked home from school and of course felt sorry for a violin thrown in a skip, no matter how terrible it might be, but when I pulled it out of the rubble I knew at once it was something special. I knew nothing about what makes a violin valuable but I could feel it through my fingers. Something made lovingly and with care feels different from something made by machine. Something old glows in a way that something new doesn't. It's not one characteristic but a thousand – a thousand tiny stars slowly forming themselves into a constellation.

I look at Matthew's message one more time.

I'm nowhere

I haven't answered it. I don't know what the right answer would be, or if there is one.

19

We eat lunch late. I order a chicken club sandwich on white toast and it arrives with toothpicks holding it together. Gil asks for toasted ham, cheese and tomato. We both get little white paper tubs of coleslaw. Like most meals in America, my sandwich is gigantic. I give up less than halfway through and wrap it up in a napkin for Honey. Gil says my eyes are bigger than my stomach and that all these leftovers are making the poor dog ill. Like this has nothing to do with him.

The waitress says she likes my accent and wants to know where we're from.

London, I say, and she says, London, England? You're so lucky to come from a place like that, and I think, she's right, I am lucky.

It's getting late and we should set off soon. As I sip lemonade out of a tall glass, I look outside and nearly choke.

Dad, I say, and point.

Oh my god, Gil mutters. It's April.

The waitress catches this last comment. Nothing at all strange about snow in April, she says. Had a blizzard at Easter once that shut down the whole state for nearly a month. Which is saying something around here. Nobody blinks about snow in April. June, you might get a few surprised looks. You might. Or you might not.

But it's been so warm.

She shrugs.

Holey Moley and Heavens to Betsy, Gil says.

The waitress doesn't notice this departure from regulation BBC English but I throw him a look. Don't turn native on me now, I whisper when she's gone. You're my last link to normality.

No such thing, he whispers back, raising an eyebrow.

You're the best I've got.

Ditto, says he.

We pay for lunch and go out to fetch the car.

Hey, Cat I text. **It's snowing! Get over here fast!**

And she bleeps back almost at once, **Wish I cud**, which I can't help reading as fairly mournful. But at least it's an answer, so maybe she's not not-talking to me after all.

The snow isn't sticking but it's whirling down so thick and soft that it's only a matter of time. We set off at a crawl and for once I don't blame Gil. He doesn't much like driving in any weather much less this weather and his face is nearly pressed to the windscreen in an attempt to see. I get the feeling we'll be up to our eyeballs quite soon but in the meantime I like the way it sweeps sideways and then straight up, not actually *falling*. You can squint at it and pretend you're in a snow globe.

It takes more than an hour to reach the cabin and by the time we arrive the world is covered over white with no sign of it stopping.

There's a little red car parked just where we parked this morning. Gil and I look at each other. We stop next to it, and I get out and brush the snow off the windows. Peering in, I see a pair of shoes in the back seat, hiking boots in a small size, a box with book CDs in it (*Anna Karenina* read by a posh actress) and greatest hits of James Taylor. Plus a bag of dried apple rings. I'd call it 100 per cent female except for a dark-blue baseball cap on the back seat with a Mets logo, which looks distinctly male.

I don't think it's Matthew, I say to Gil, and he nods.

Honey jumps out of the car and lands gingerly in the snow without looking particularly surprised. Once again, I'm wondering how Matthew left Honey behind. He obviously knows how Suzanne feels about his dog, knows she won't be lavishing Honey with affection and care. Which makes his leaving her even stranger. He loves her. He must, given how much she loves him. Has he gone somewhere he couldn't take a dog? On a plane?

Come on, says Gil, pulling his jacket around him and tucking his chin down into the collar. We head down the path once more. A bit more hesitantly this time, in case folks round these parts shoot first and ask questions later. You never know with Americans.

Hello! calls Gil when we get to the clearing, and I hope someone answers soon because my shoes are soaked and my hair has begun to drip. If the snow decides to stick around for any length of time, I'm going to have to kit up.

The door is closed but there are lights on, and I can see grey smoke climbing out of the chimney. A woman comes to the door and looks out at us. Her expression is puzzled and for an instant the same thought flashes through my head and Gil's: we're at the wrong house.

She's wearing a denim apron over a long skirt and a heavy dark-blue Norwegian sweater with white flecks in it. She wipes her hands and stares out at us.

Honey stands close beside me, the snow landing but not melting on her coat. She's leaning a little on my leg. I'm watching and watching and even though it's only seconds in real life, time slows down so it feels like ages.

All of a sudden the woman raises one hand to her mouth, flings open the door and runs out into the snow to embrace Gil, who hugs her back.

What in god's name are you doing here? You're getting wet, she laughs. Don't just stand there, come in, come in!

When she unhugs him at last, she turns to me and I notice that her eyes are slanted up at the outside, like a cat's, so it's Mila-dog meets anonymous-cat and I wonder if we're going to bristle at each other and she's going to hunch up her back and start hissing, but she just grabs Gil's arm and mine, and half-drags us inside out of the cold.

Then she stands and looks at Gil, at me, back to Gil.

Mila, says Gil, this is Lynda. A very old friend of mine and Matthew's. From way before you were born.

Lynda smiles. About a century ago, she says.

We stand there, the three of us, Gil and I dripping on the floor of her tiny house, Lynda looking at Gil as if she can't get enough of him. At last she breaks the spell, hurrying off to a chest of drawers from which she pulls an armful of towels. Dry your hair, she says, handing me a blue one, or you'll catch cold.

It's so warm in the cabin that we start to steam. Gil ruffles my hair with his towel and I ask Lynda if it's OK to use mine to dry Honey, who's snuffling around every nook and cranny like we're playing Find the Rabbit.

She's not dirty or smelly, I say, and Lynda says, Of course she's not.

What a crazy day, she says. Snow! At Easter. And now you turning up out of the blue, Gil, how completely – she stops, searching for a word strong enough to do justice to it all – *astonishing*.

I catch Honey and when I'm done drying her, she gives a big dog-shake in an attempt to unruffle her fur, and I look at Lynda. She's younger than Gil, her hair shoulder length and dark with hardly any grey in it and she's tall. It occurs to me that she could possibly be the girl in the picture from so long ago, the girl they both loved, and I wonder if Matthew is keeping her hidden away up here like Rapunzel in a tower.

Gil just stares at her. Well, he says. You'd better tell me what you're doing here.

I've been living here since we came back from Scotland. Nearly three years ago. What on earth are *you* doing here?

We're searching for Matthew, says Gil. You heard he disappeared?

What? Lynda blinks. What do you mean, disappeared? How would I have heard?

He set off a few days ago, taking nothing special with him, no money, passport, clothes. Just his car. And that was it. He didn't come home. We thought he might have come here.

He didn't, she says. We haven't seen him in months. And she opens her palms in a gesture that suggests we look around under the bed or in the drawers if we don't believe her.

OK, so…*we haven't seen him in months.* Which suggests *we* did see him before that? And by the way, I'm thinking, who's *we?* I suppose it could be another man, currently hiding in the woods, but there's a T-shirt draped on the back of a chair with the name of a band on it, an empty box of M&Ms in the bin and a plate on the floor with the remains of breakfast, all of which suggests some version of kid.

Gil sighs and then seems aware that he's being ungracious. Never mind, he says. As surprises go, I couldn't ask for a nicer one.

You're shameless, Lynda smiles. But it's lovely to see you. And Mila! She drags her attention away from my father. That's the trouble with break-ups, she says. You lose everyone else too. But your father and I always got along. I always suspected I chose the wrong friend.

Break-ups. The wrong friend. So she *is* the girl in the photograph.

Lynda smiles again and gives me a look to show that she's not serious about the wrong-friend thing, though it strikes me with some force that she is.

I check Gil to confirm this impression and yes, there is something. My father is attracted to this woman, this old girlfriend of Matthew's. I narrow my eyes, but neither of them is looking at me.

Matt didn't tell you I was living here?

Gil shakes his head. We're not great at keeping in touch. Even less since Owen died. The occasional email, not much else. Suzanne thought he might have come here. Gil looks anxious. You know he's married?

Of course.

But Suzanne doesn't know about this arrangement?

I never asked, says Lynda. But on the evidence, it would appear not.

Even with my lack of worldly knowledge, this strikes me as a bad idea. Should Matthew be keeping this sort of secret? And why, exactly, is their relationship such a secret if she was his girlfriend a hundred years ago?

Look, Lynda says, please sit down, sit down. Let me get you something warm to drink. You must be freezing.

It's warm in here and we aren't freezing, but we both sit at the wooden gateleg table and watch as she heats coffee and milk on her little gas stove.

I teach English at the local high school, she says. Doesn't pay fabulously but they like me. Matt visits occasionally and sends money though I tell him not to. I keep meaning to move into a more sensible house but he doesn't charge us to live here. Basic as it is, that counts for something.

I glance at Gil, who acts as if there's nothing wrong with this picture. We just happen to be here in Matthew's cabin with his secret ex-girlfriend + one, who Matthew sends money to and doesn't charge rent, and none of this has any bearing on our mystery?

Lynda bends down and puts her hand out to Honey, who is stand-offish and withdraws as much as possible without moving her feet. Most dogs would sniff the hand.

She's Matt's dog, Gil says. Her name is Honey.

Lynda nods. I thought so. We've met, actually.

Gil's eyes widen for an instant. Of course you have, he says. But he looks wrong-footed.

Honey backs away and resumes sniffing every corner of

the room. Every once in a while she stops and tries to inhale a particular object. Matthew may not have been here for some time, but Honey's sense of smell is a lot better than mine. The house remembers him, whispering his name at a frequency only dogs can hear.

And then she stops, having collected all the information available. She's still damp, Lynda says, digging around in the bottom of a drawer and pulling out an old grey blanket. She puts it down by the stove and Honey steps over carefully, sniffing to make sure there's no trick, then turns in a circle and lies down. Maybe the blanket smells of Matthew too.

So. Lynda frowns at Gil. Why exactly have you got Matt's dog?

It's kind of a long story, he says.

He left her behind? That's not like him.

Gil sighs.

Unless he was going somewhere he can't take a dog?

We kind of hoped he'd be here. But you're right.

Could he have gone back to England?

We have no idea, Gil says. Though why would he? When he knew we were coming.

Lynda says nothing, setting coffee on the table for Gil and hot chocolate for me.

Gil and I are both trying to take all this in and Gil looks at me questioningly. I shrug and wonder how much he sees and whether he thinks Matthew has been here recently. I have as many questions as he does. Maybe Matthew is having an affair with Lynda and just visits occasionally? Is she the reason he disappeared? And, if so, where is he now?

I look around. Bowls and saucepans are cordoned off in

the kitchen corner with the tiny old-fashioned gas cooker. On the other side, corduroy cushions are piled next to a collection of duck decoys, two ancient folding chairs, and piles of books. It's just one rectangular room, divided into sections that confirm the idea that more than one person lives here. The partition wall at one end must have a bed behind it, and a large grey sofa takes up most of the middle of the room along with a small desk pushed against the wall and a scarred leather armchair. The floor is almost entirely covered by an old Persian rug, faded and threadbare. Lynda has arranged a bunch of lily of the valley in a glass by the window and the sweet smell of it fills the house. She must have picked them before the weather turned psycho.

Lynda slides half a carrot cake on to a large blue-and-white plate and says she's glad we're there to help her eat it.

Despite it being the wilds of northern New York State, you wouldn't know it by the sound of our little group of three representing Scotland, Lancashire and London.

So he's disappeared, Lynda says thoughtfully, and then looks up at Gil, a bit hesitant. He's done it before, you know.

What?

Gil frowns. No, I didn't know.

After Owen died. He walked out of the hospital and no one heard from him for two days. I guess under the circumstances you might expect a person to do something crazy.

Gil looks suitably shocked. Well, he says, yes. But it wouldn't be everyone's choice. Especially when it meant leaving Suzanne alone.

How horrible, I think. What a cruel thing to do.

At the inquest, he couldn't account for those days, couldn't remember where he'd been or what he'd done. We were still in Scotland, but I read about it online.

I look at Gil. *He's disappeared before and Suzanne didn't mention it?* Gil's expression hasn't changed.

It must have been so terrible for him, Lynda says. I always thought he was the world's kindest man.

Unless you're his wife, left alone for two days with a dead son. I refrain from saying this out loud.

Lynda's tone changes again. When you say disappeared, Gil . . . has he run away *to* somewhere? *With* someone? How do you know he's not having an affair or –?

Dead, she means.

Oh, says Gil, I'm pretty sure he's alive. I'm guessing he just needed to be away for a bit. You know what he's like.

Lynda looks doubtful. Yes, but to walk off like that without a word. Not even a note? She frowns. Making everyone worry. Dragging you over from London and all.

We'd planned the visit some time ago, Gil says.

Lynda stares at him, puts her hand on his arm. But that's even worse. Surely it's not just coincidence?

Gil shrugs. You think he didn't want to see me? After all this time? He sounded pleased when I said we were coming.

It can't be coincidence, Lynda says. But why wouldn't he want to see you?

Lynda's right, I think. It doesn't strike me as the act of a rational man who just needs a bit of space, which is how Gil interprets it. People who need to get away don't drop everything and disappear just when their long-lost friend is coming three thousand miles to visit.

Has he been in touch with Oliver? Gil asks.

I don't think so.

Gil addresses me now. Lynda's brother, Oliver, he says, pleasantly and for my information (as if we were not just four seconds ago discussing his oldest friend's strange-possibly-desperate behaviour) and Matt were at university together. That's how they met. Oliver introduced them.

I was living with another woman, Lynda says, also to me.

How fascinating, Lynda, I think. Possibly not entirely pertinent, however. What is it with this woman? All of a sudden she and Gil are talking as if they're an old married couple and I'm some jolly house guest.

Do you remember her, Gil?

He nods. Of course.

Lynda turns towards me so as not to make me feel left out, but it's Gil she's addressing.

She was one of those old-fashioned, men are the enemy, all-sex-is-rape type of lesbians. Well, what did I know. I was young.

I stare at her, telegraphing that I am entirely uninterested in the details of her sex life, past or present. There is more than enough for me to absorb here without extraneous facts. And by the way, Lynda, do you think you might stop flirting with my dad?

Anyway. Lynda smiles. It took me decades to get it right.

Gil looks at her. But you have now?

I hope so. One of my colleagues at school.

That's good to hear. Some people never get it right.

You did though.

I've been lucky, Gil says.

She laughs. You've always been lucky. I am just so glad to lay eyes on you, even for an hour or two. And Mila. I've missed you. Really I have.

She beams at us both but I'm sincerely doubting that she's missed me.

The front door opens.

What now? Matthew? Lynda's lesbian lover? Marley's ghost?

Jake! Is it still snowing? Come say hello to Matthew's old friend – my old friend – this is Gil and his daughter, Mila. She points to me as a tall, dark-haired boy of about fifteen with brown eyes and a big blue puffa jacket shuffles through the door. This is my son, says Lynda. Get something to eat and come sit, Jake.

Hold on a minute. Why would Matthew send money to his ex-girlfriend and her son? Unless. Is it possible that Jake is also Matthew's son? Is that why Matthew sends money? Or is he just helping out an old friend? Do people send money to needy ex-girlfriends? I look at Gil and wonder if he's keeping up with what Lynda's saying or has utterly failed to absorb the information coming our way.

Quick-wittedness can be very lonely.

Lynda keeps talking like there's nothing at all weird about a sometimes lesbian, who may or may not be the mother of Gil's best friend's secret teenage son, flirting with my father. I feel dizzy.

He sent me an announcement when Gabriel was born, she's saying, sweeping her hair up off her neck and holding it in a bunch behind her head. I was happy for them. Matt said Suzanne wanted another child even before Owen.

She means before Owen died, but won't say it. And what about Matt? Did he want another child?

We all fall silent, though I have less falling to do than the others, my contribution consisting mainly of gaping with incomprehension. Honey lies quietly beside me, head on paws, eyes open, watching. I wish she and I could compare notes.

I'm sorry we can't help you, Lynda says. We would if we could.

Don't worry, Gil answers. It was a long shot that we'd find him here.

I look at him. As far as I'm concerned it was our shortest and only shot.

Where will you look next?

I've no idea, says Gil. We were pretty much gambling on this place.

Lynda looks from Gil to me, her face anxious. Jake has made himself a sandwich and flopped down on the sofa to eat it. I turn round to look at him and he meets my eyes as if noticing for the first time that I'm here. Hi, he says.

Hi.

This is Mila, says Lynda. Gil's daughter. Gil is an old friend of Matthew's.

You said that, Jake says.

I'm looking at Jake and wondering what his line is on his maybe-father, whether he dislikes him for being married to someone else and hiding Jake's existence from his new family. Assuming he has. And Jake is.

But hold on a minute. Let's say that Jake is actually Matthew's son and *is* actually around fifteen, then isn't he pretty much the same age Owen would be? I'm twelve and a half, and Owen and I were born three years and three days apart.

So Matthew couldn't possibly be his father. Unless . . . oh god.

Use a plate, Lynda says to Jake, and picks one up from a shelf behind the table. I take it from her and she thanks me, then turns back to Gil. I really do wish I could help. But I don't have any idea where he might be. I don't even know who his friends are.

I walk over to the sofa with the plate and look down at Jake. How old are you? I ask him, and he looks a bit nonplussed. It's a somewhat strange conversation-opener but I have to know.

Fifteen, Lynda says from across the room. Last September.

September? And he's fifteen? Owen was born in October. My theory must be wrong. It would mean Lynda got pregnant about the same time as Suzanne, by the same man. Do people even *do* things like that?

It would certainly explain why Suzanne doesn't know they're staying here. I stare at Jake but he's taken the plate from me, smiled politely, replaced his earphones, half closed his eyes and switched his concentration inward.

Across the room, Gil and Lynda are still talking.

I walk back to my chair and sit down. Gil smiles at me. He is probably experiencing regrets for his friend and Lynda and the relationship between them that didn't work out, and not concentrating on the big story at all. I blink at him in a meaningful way, but he merely looks puzzled.

It's starting to get dark and Lynda gets up to light oil lamps in glass hurricane shades. Jake has somehow managed to disappear in this tiny house, still stretched out on the sofa, eyes closed, plugged in to his iPod. I need to use the toilet and when I ask if it's OK, Lynda hands me Jake's big puffa jacket and a torch. Do you want me to come out with you? The snow is quite heavy.

But I know where to go and I'm desperate to be alone for a few minutes to clear my head. The coat feels nice, light and warm and smelling of boy. Honey follows silently as I pick my way across the new snow. The door creaks a little when I open it and it's cold in here, but I'm cosy in my cocoon and the wooden seat is wide and smooth. Honey squeezes into the tiny room beside me, not wanting to be left out in the snow. She presses up against my legs and I sit down, grateful beyond words to be away from that house full of silent drama.

I do the maths once more to be absolutely certain, but it just adds up the same. Barring premature births, if Jake is Matthew's son, he was conceived the same month as Owen.

Despite the turmoil in my head, sitting in the dark with only the torch is quite a nice feeling. Peaceful. I switch it on and make slow circles on the walls, thinking. I'm completely warm inside the jacket with Honey leaning up against my legs. Something about the warm coat and the cold air and the dark and the quiet and the strangeness and all the revelations of the past half hour make me want to sit here forever. I feel almost drowsy staring at the swirls of light I'm making on the wall, turning my brain away by force from the confusion in it and wondering how Lynda and Jake manage in winter when there's tons of snow. Could you even get to the toilet or would it be buried? I shudder. And who would clear the road? In London when it snows, everything shuts down. Maybe Lynda went back to Scotland in order for Jake to be born as far away from Matthew and Suzanne as possible. Under the circumstances, I can see her point.

I wonder why they came back, and to so primitive a place.

Eventually my feet start to feel cold so I get up and open the door, then jump back with my heart flipping over in my chest because there's a dark shape looming near a tree about ten feet away and I'm about to scream and run when I realize that bears don't wear boots and sweaters, and as bears go, this one looks a lot like Jake.

I'm here to make sure you haven't got lost in the woods and frozen to death, he says.

What about getting scared to death?

Sorry, he says. What on earth were you doing in there all that time, if you don't mind my asking? He rubs his hands together and blows on them, watching me.

Well, this is embarrassing, but at least it's too dark for him to see. I was just thinking, I tell him, and even in the dark I can see him roll his eyes.

Come on, he says, and grabs a handful of my jacket. No one cares if I freeze to death while you sit around in the cold thinking. But his tone isn't annoyed; it's actually quite nice and friendly.

He and Honey and I shuffle back through the snow in single file. White smoke is curling out of the little tin chimney. Back inside, Lynda's built up the fire. The cosiness of the place probably makes up for a lot of inconvenience. It smells of wood smoke. I wonder how the two of them can live here. There's not exactly a lot of privacy.

Found her, says Jake, flopping down on the sofa once more and slipping his earphones back on. Honey surprises me by padding over to him. She lies down on the floor beside him and he reaches down to stroke her.

She's an old girl, isn't she? Lynda says, looking at them. I guess she got left behind too? Honey makes a rumbling noise in her chest and I look at her and Jake.

Once more I wonder: Why would he leave Honey?

I'm afraid we'd better go, Gil says, peering out at the snow.

He's worried about finding his way back with no visibility and all the road signs covered in snow. What he ought to be worried about is the countless surprising revelations Lynda's sprung on us.

Will you come again? At least let me make you lunch tomorrow. Lynda has one hand on my arm, though I suspect it's Gil she'd rather arm-hold.

Even though I know we haven't got all the time in the world and the roads will be completely covered in snow and we have flights back to London and need to find Matthew, I know before Gil says anything that we'll be coming back tomorrow for lunch. Though to be fair, where else can we go?

What about the roads? I ask, feeling obscurely resentful.

I guess we just wait and see what it looks like in the morning, says Gil.

We say goodbye to Lynda, who gives me a hug and tells us to drive carefully. I'll try and contact Matt tonight, she says, though I doubt he'll answer my calls if he hasn't answered yours.

Jake doesn't get up, though his mum grumbles at him for being rude, so he waves at us from the sofa and then shuts his eyes again.

Despite all the strange quasi-revelations, I can't bring myself to dislike Jake and Lynda. They seem half like displaced people waiting for something to happen and half like woodland creatures who've always lived here. I'm guessing that Lynda's lonely for people who've known her a long time, or maybe just someone who doesn't live plugged into an iPod. Perhaps Gil isn't acting in anything more than the friendly manner of a person who was once fond of another person.

Seeing them together, I get a funny feeling that Lynda, Jake and Honey have all been discarded in Matthew's wake. Once again, I wonder what sort of person Matthew must be to walk out on the people who love him.

I take out the phone to reply to his text.

Matthew

I stare at the single word for a long time, wondering what else I can possibly say. It is impossible to put into a text everything I want to know. Where are you? Why did you go? Do Jake and Lynda have anything to do with all this? Why did you leave Honey behind? And perhaps most urgently, What happened to your life?

Instead, I write: **Is Jake your son?**

I leave the message as it is and press send, but I can't help noticing that the people in his orbit are beginning, slowly, to add up. Suzanne, Gabriel, Owen, Jake, Lynda, Honey. All circling some sort of story that only Matthew can see completely.

As for Gil and me? We're searching for Matthew but keep finding other things.

20

My own next of kin has some explaining to do.

But, he protests, think about it. I didn't have the faintest clue we were going to run into Lynda. She didn't seem especially relevant when we set off. I haven't seen or heard from her – haven't thought about her – in years. And Matthew somehow never got around to telling me about Jake, *if* in fact Jake is his son and Matt isn't just sending money to Lynda for any of a hundred other reasons.

A hundred? Name one.

You know what I mean.

I guess you couldn't just ask?

Gil looks uncomfortable. I suppose. But wouldn't she have told us if she wanted us to know?

Maybe she thinks you know already. Being Matthew's best friend and all.

Of course, if it's true, it's quite shocking, Gil says, frowning. I wonder if Suzanne knows. Do you think he'd have told her?

Do *I* think? I'm twelve.

Gil smiles. Yes, of course. I keep forgetting.

Uh huh. I don't say anything but, just on the fly, I'm guessing he didn't tell Suzanne.

This whole story gets messier and messier, says Gil, and he sounds weary all of a sudden. There's Matt's disappearance after the accident as well.

Why would he do that?

Gil shakes his head. I have no idea.

It's very snowy and he is concentrating on not sliding into other cars. There's so much going on in my own head that I don't know where to start. It feels as if the landscape has cracked open to reveal a river of lava flowing beneath.

Gil pulls in at the Mountain View Motor Inn, which is undergoing that strange kind of transformation that happens when a completely alien place begins to feel like home. First you say, I'd like to go *home* now, or, Let's go *home*, and suddenly realize that you don't mean your lifelong home in London, but the Mountain View Motor Inn.

The motel is nice inside with huge comfortable beds. Gil plugs his computer into the converter plug from the airport and reaches down to find the socket. The manuscript of the book he is translating covers most of his bed, and the book he found in the second-hand shop sits on a pillow like Cinderella's glass slipper.

I liked the idea that there was no one but me in Gil's life at the moment, but Lynda and Jake and the ghosts of Matthew and Owen have all crowded in on the party and ruined the illusion. It is very weird to see your father look at another woman as a woman, even if it is completely harmless. It is also fairly strange to discover that your father's best friend may have been cheating on his wife about the same time he got her pregnant.

Gil says a bit peevishly that he's not getting any work done, which is hardly surprising given the circumstances.

Never mind, I say, it's only a few days. Try to enjoy the company.

He kisses my forehead and replies, How could I not?

Lynda seems nice, I say cautiously.

Yes, he says. She is. But her life is messy, as ever.

I think about this. What do you mean?

Oh, well, he says. If it wasn't one thing it was another. Two men. A woman and a man. Always some combination that didn't quite work. I found it intriguing years ago – now it just makes me feel tired.

Do you think Matthew knew she was pregnant?

You're making a huge assumption here, Mila. It's only a theory.

But what if I'm right?

Gil shrugs. Who knows? But he does send them money. If you're right, then it would appear he found out eventually.

I look at him. Tell me, I say, is there some huge adult conspiracy where people lead unimaginably complex lives and pretend it's normal?

No such thing as –

I cut him off. *Don't say it.*

He sighs. But don't you see? It's possible to make one mistake, which leads to more and bigger mistakes until you can't find your way back. And then you drag other people in and the complications escalate. Life can get messy very quickly. And Matt's always been quite an individual sort of a person.

What does that mean?

He was always happiest on his own. On a rock face, away from the world. Not a domestic paragon like me, he says. Now go to bed. He gives me his stern look, kisses me and goes back to work.

I send one last text under the covers.

Please tell me why you left.

No answer comes. I fall asleep and the snow tries to bury us in the night.

The nice waitress at our breakfast place isn't on duty next morning. Of course, Gil says, it's Saturday. The new waitress is a friendly girl with fair hair pulled back in a ponytail. She has a slightly displaced air and I decide she followed some boyfriend up to this place and then got stranded. A wild guess.

I skip the muffins, pancakes and waffles, spinach omelettes, smoothies and smoked salmon bagels in favour of toast and orange juice. Infinite variety is beginning to wear me down.

As soon as we've finished breakfast, we start the slow drive out to Lynda's. The roads are clear, sanded and salted like they actually expect this sort of thing to happen, with massive snow piles big enough to hollow out and live in by the side of the road. I guess they do expect this sort of thing to happen.

It's still snowing, but the snow is delicate now, light and dry. The sun is shining, the sky impossibly blue. The world looks so dazzling I almost can't bear to look at it.

Even Lynda's little narrow road has been ploughed and we pull over at the usual place to park. Her car is completely covered in snow and I draw a smiley face on the windscreen with one finger. She hears our car and calls us in out of the cold.

Inside, the wood burner is throwing out masses of heat and it's cosy and sociable, but I can't help wondering if it might feel lonely and remote when we're not here.

Jake's out shovelling driveways, she tells us. He'll be back for lunch. But within minutes of our arrival he bursts in covered with snow, grinning like Tom after a hearty meal of Jerry.

I'm rich! he says, pulling out a wad of notes and throwing off his Mets cap. I hope it snows till August. He strips off his jacket and gloves and hangs them, dripping, over a chair by the fire. His mother pours him a hot chocolate.

It's hard work, and freezing out there. Gotta get my strength back. Jake slumps down in a chair and once more Honey gets up and pads over to lie next to him. He pats her absently. So, he says, how's the mystery of the missing Matthew going? Course, it's not a particularly fascinating mystery for us. He's been missing from our lives more or less, let's see, forever.

Lynda and Gil are talking quietly about other things, so I look at him, take a deep breath and say in a low voice, Is Matthew your father?

You don't exactly beat around the bush, do you? he says with half a smile. Matthew's not much of a father, but technically speaking? Yes. Didn't you know?

I shake my head. The tone Jake takes is so matter of fact

that it's impossible to figure out whether he cares. That his father is Matthew. That his father is missing. Anything. He'd be a good poker player, Jake would.

After a few minutes, he gets up to check if his things are dry and puts his cap back on. I'm going out again, he says. Do you want to come? You could make a small fortune to take back to England. Genuine American dinero. He rubs his fingers together.

Very tempting, I say.

You'll have to take my coat and boots, Lynda says, but doesn't wait for an answer, just fetches both. And a hat. I wonder if the grown-ups want to be alone.

Before I know it I'm wearing a pair of slightly too big fur-lined boots and a long down coat and a fleece hat and gloves, and Jake and I are trudging through the snow.

I feel like a hobbit, I say. Do I look like one too?

Uncannily, he says.

I have to skip a little to keep up. Don't you get freaked out living so far from everything? I look at him. I mean, what do you do around here if something happens? Don't get me wrong, it's beautiful and all, but what about, like, axe murderers and zombies?

Having lived in a city my whole life, the country feels like a horror film waiting to happen, where some crazy person is always lurking in the bushes ready to pounce.

Jake looks at me sideways. I haven't seen a zombie in weeks, he says. Or an axe murderer. There are actually tons of people around here, they just hide up at the end of little roads so you can't see them. If you chopped a tree down on top of yourself and broke both legs, you could always find someone who'd stuff you into the back of a pick-up and ferry you to the hospital. Of course, afterwards they'd tell everyone in town what an incompetent moron you are.

There doesn't seem to be an obvious answer to this.

I like your accent by the way, he says as we trudge along, and I laugh.

What's funny? He shifts the shovels to his other shoulder.

Nothing, it's just that everyone says that. It doesn't sound like an accent to me. You're the one with the accent.

Me? Jake snorts. I grew up in Scotland but I thought I sounded American now.

You do. Almost.

Almost? He feigns outrage. I've won awards for my American accent.

Really? I stop and look at him. Awards?

Well, no. Not actual awards.

I'd give you an award, I say. I like the way you sound.

Thank you, he says. Very kind.

We trudge along for another few minutes. So what do we do, just go up to perfect strangers' doors and ask for a job?

That's it, he says. Only we use careful scientific methods to figure out if they're likely to hire us.

Like if the drive is covered in snow?

Yup.

And that's what we do. The only hitch is getting to the end of all the little roads before we find out if they might need us. We do lots of backtracking but finally we ring the bell of a house with snow on the driveway and Jake makes me talk because of my cool accent, and the woman who answers the door offers us less than the going rate, but Jake says she's kind of old so we'll be doing a good deed. She gives us the money and we take her little dog out for a walk as well, and she seems really grateful. But it's hard work and my arms are killing me after just one job.

Anyone who's not dug out by now, Jake says, is going to be either old or away or a husband-free zone. Which turns out to be true, because all the people who answer the door are either over seventy or women you can't quite imagine wearing snow boots and doing manual labour. We're out for three hours and get two more jobs.

There's not much talk while we're working because it takes all my energy just to throw the snow around.

It's not particularly heavy, Jake says, which is great because they don't pay you any more for wet snow and we'd both be dead of exhaustion by now. Or at least you would be.

I'm kind of getting into the rhythm of shovelling, though my shoulders are killing me. Dig, toss. Dig, toss. When I get tired of tossing I try to kick the back of the shovel to move the snow over, but Jake says there's no point, it just gets packed up hard and more difficult to move when the time comes to clear it. He sends me over to the front path, but it's started snowing once more, so by the time I clear the whole thing it's turning white again.

Everyone's got sand and salt, so we salt first and sand afterwards, collect our money and go on to the next.

You're a good worker, Jake says. I knew you would be.

What, do I look like a lady weightlifter or something? I flex my arm, but the effect is muffled by three inches of padded coat.

He grins. Nah. You don't look that strong. But you're not the complaining type.

Totally untrue, I say. Complaining's one of my best things. Right now I'm starving and cold and really sick of the sight of snow.

Yeah, he says, me too. Let's go home.

Jake divides the money up as we walk along and hands me half. It looks like a fortune. Yikes, I say. Do you think I could buy a house around here with this?

He nods. At least one.

We walk in silence for a minute. So what do you think of Matthew disappearing? I ask him. The minute I've said it, I wish I hadn't. I've already got a reputation for blunt questions.

But he answers. I've met him a bunch of times since we've been here, he says, but I don't exactly know him well. Before that we'd see him once a year or every other year. I like him enough, but he's always quite formal with me. Do you want my theory? I haven't got one. Maybe he's got twelve sons like me hidden away and he can't stand the guilt. He stops and looks at me. What's your theory?

This is not an easy question to answer. I don't know enough to have a theory, I tell him. I don't know anything about him, really. I pause. And you've made the story even more confusing. Do you think his wife knows about you and your mum?

I doubt it, Jake says. It's weird being someone's dirty secret. That's one thing I don't like about the whole deal. He shrugs. But I'm used to it.

Really? I don't say anything to Jake, but I can see that it would be weird. Horrible, even, and I'm hating Matthew more with every new thing I know about him. Why are we searching for this man? Why is he my father's friend?

It's not really fair, I say.

He looks at me. When I leave home I get to choose. I've already decided I'm moving back to Scotland when I can. I liked it. Except in winter, when it's dark most of the time.

How long did you live there?

My whole life till I was twelve, he says. Mum worked in New York City for a while. That's how she kept in touch with Matthew. When she found out she was pregnant, she decided to move closer to her sister, in Aberdeen. But she and her sister never got along all that well, how funny is that? Anyway, she got her teaching qualification and decided to move back. I think she likes it better here.

What about you?

We lived on a big council estate over there. It was OK. There was a decent skate park. And thousands of kids. I liked it. The social life around here isn't exactly riveting.

You're sounding Scottish all of a sudden.

I'm not.

You *are*.

He looks away but I can tell he's pleased.

So far, nothing earth-shattering has happened between us, but just talking about anything can be big when you're on the same wavelength. I've noticed that the magic of getting on with someone isn't really magic. If you break it down, you can see how it happens. You say something a bit off-centre and see if they react. If they get it, they push it a bit further. Then it's your turn again. And theirs. And so on, until it's banter. Once it's banter, it's friendship.

We open the door to the cabin and across the room talking to Gil is a slim woman in her forties with short red hair and neat features, wearing an expensive-looking suit. She looks almost weirdly fashionable for someone in a snowstorm in the middle of nowhere.

This is my friend, Joy, says Lynda. She offers no other explanation, filling the space where an explanation might have gone by bustling around with our wet things and more hot drinks.

The girlfriend, says Jake in a low voice.

Oh.

Lynda hands us cocoa and she and Joy go back to telling Gil about their school and how teachers have to spend so much time with paperwork, and that's where I tune out.

Given how many people have now squashed into this little place, Jake's sofa has become a kind of refuge. He must think so too cos he pulls up his knees to make room for me and after a minute hands me one of his earphones.

Good song, I say.

He nods. Not famous yet, but someday you'll be able to tell everyone you heard it here first, on the somethingth day of something, two thousand and something, on my sofa right here. It'll be just like the first time your parents ever heard the Beatles.

I find it hard to imagine that Gil remembers where he first heard the Beatles, or maybe even who the Beatles are. His radar for popular culture is, shall we say, imperfect.

Who's the singer? I ask, and he looks hurt.

Oh my god! I say, realizing. That's amazing! You've got a totally amazing voice. (This happens to be true.)

I write songs with my friend Chris.

Oh, I think. Chris boy or Chris girl?

I have to squinch up if we're going to share the same earphones and he makes room for me at his end and before long we're sitting squashed up together like it's the most natural thing in the world.

Jake is friendly but a little reserved. I think Honey likes him for the same reasons I do.

Lynda's nodding in our direction, like, isn't it nice that they get on, but Gil thinks she's pointing at the still-life painting on the shelf above us, which happens to be one of Joy's so the conversation veers off. I stifle a laugh.

What are you going to do now? Lynda asks Gil, and I tune in immediately, aware that I've missed a lot of conversation while we were out. I've only got one earphone, which is useful for eavesdropping.

Gil shrugs. Still no plan B. Back to Suzanne's, I guess. Not much else we can do unless we hear from him. Gil is slicing cucumber for the salad while Lynda lays the table and Joy opens a beer, which she offers to Gil.

You know, Gil says, I've been wondering why Matthew disappeared after the car accident.

For possibly the first time in his long, eventful life, my father has asked the right question. But the question has caused a definite atmospheric shift, and it makes me think they haven't brought up the subject of Matthew today at all. I'm watching Joy now, who hasn't said a word but is clearly about to.

Lynda glances at her uneasily, then back at Gil.

The reason he disappeared, Joy says, with exaggerated

calm, is that he's a total shit who doesn't know the first thing about responsibility or commitment.

Lynda looks away, but Joy is just warming up.

He's a loner, that's his problem. And he doesn't give a damn about anyone but himself.

You know that's not true. Lynda casts an anxious glance in her son's direction, but Jake appears able to blank everything beyond the confines of his personal space.

Gil looks from Joy to Lynda.

I've known Matthew a long time, Gil begins, but Joy interrupts.

Look at his track record, she says, nearly spitting the words. One dead son, one abandoned. He left his girlfriend, cheated on his wife, now he's left her *and* the baby –

That's enough, says Lynda in a quiet voice, and it's clear that this is not the first time Joy's opinion has been aired.

It's not, actually, enough, Joy says in a clipped voice. Of course, *I've* never met the man, never been hypnotized into thinking he's some kind of hero who just *happens* to ruin the lives of everyone he comes in contact with, so what would *I* know?

Gil glances at me but I pretend to be immersed in Jake's music.

She likes this line of discourse, Jake whispers, close to my ear.

I nod. It's pretty uncomfortable on that side of the house, what with Joy all pursed up and cross and Lynda's desire for everyone to play nice. But over on our side it's kind of cosy. What I like about Jake is how much he observes and how little any of it seems to ruffle his feathers. It's like he's taken the entire adult world on board and decided it's mildly amusing and mildly irrelevant.

He taps my knee and I look at him sideways. Anyway, he whispers, back to the original question about why Matthew disappeared after the car crash? He makes an imaginary glass with one hand, tips it into his mouth, then closes his eyes and goes back to the music.

Matthew was *drinking*?

My mind races. He was *drinking*? Did he drink a *lot*? Did Lynda and Matthew's relationship break up because Matthew drank? Or Matthew and Suzanne's? But wait, if he'd been drinking on the day of the accident, then of course he disappeared right after. He needed to disappear till all the signs were gone or he'd go to jail for murdering his son. If he had been drinking that day, the guilt would eat away at him for the rest of his life. What more would a person need to go off the rails? Or run away? Or even kill himself? Or does Jake mean he started drinking after the accident? Went on a bender? I look at Jake, trying to ask my questions via psychic transfer, but his eyes are closed, his expression serene.

Joy is in the process of struggling into her coat.

Don't go, Lynda says, but she doesn't sound very convincing.

Nice meeting you, Joy says to Gil as she opens the door. Hope you find what you're looking for.

She lets herself out and the door bangs shut behind her.

Lynda looks at Gil. Sorry about that, she says. Matt's not her favourite person. She thinks she's protecting me, I guess. Though I wish she wouldn't.

Gil waves a dismissive hand. Yes, of course, of course. But

Joy's outburst has shaken him. Perhaps he never looked at Matthew objectively. Perhaps the Matthew he remembers is out of date.

Lynda sighs. Maybe you should tell the police.

I am taken aback, until I realize that my brain has rushed on to a whole new story. Lynda's talking about finding a missing person and I've jumped to an alcoholic child killer.

The police aren't interested, says Gil. Adults don't get to be missing persons in the eyes of the law unless they leave a suicide note or a trail of blood. Otherwise it's assumed they just wanted to be somewhere else. Which in this case is probably true.

He's walked out on another child, Lynda says quietly, as if the reality has just occurred to her.

That makes two, Gil says.

Three. Her voice is quiet.

It's not a great track record.

No, Lynda says. It's crap, actually. For the first time she doesn't sound gentle and tolerant, and I'm wondering what happened to everyone's best friend, the kindest man in the world.

Looking at Lynda, I can see that old relationships leave a flare behind them, an uneven tail of light that doesn't go away when people split up.

I remove my one earphone to hear better and Jake leans in close.

Stop listening, he whispers. It's. Not. Polite.

I poke him. He pokes me back, and then we're struggling half-on half-off the sofa, and I'm laughing so hard I can hardly breathe. You win, I gasp, and replace the earphone.

Lunch, kids, says Lynda.

Jake and I get to our feet a little sheepishly and shuffle over to the table together, still plugged in.

Off, says Lynda, pointing, and I hand him back his earphone. The lunch Lynda serves is nice: beef stew with white beans and salad.

The last thing I expected was to find a person like Jake here in the middle of nowhere, but aside from him, this whole story is starting to make me angry. All these people flung around on the end of a rope because one man keeps on making problems and running away. Or at least that's what it looks like from where I'm sitting.

While Lynda's clearing up, I wrap myself in Jake's big down jacket and step outside for a bit of privacy, and to write one more text.

What happened on the day Owen died?

I stare at the phone and press send. It is not a question I would ever dare ask in person. But in the absence of anyone else getting to the bottom of this mystery I have started to feel a bit desperate.

The little ping of the message flying off calms me. When I go back inside, Jake gives me a look. My father is shaking out his coat in preparation for our departure. I feel suddenly sad.

Jake takes my UK and US mobile numbers and my email and says he'll have to keep in touch with me because otherwise I won't know anything about cutting-edge bands back in my sad little English hick town.

You should come and visit, Gil says. London's not so bad really.

Yeah, come, I say, and Lynda says, Maybe this summer.

We all hug and kiss, even Jake, and everyone feels happy to have met and sad to be parting so soon.

Lynda and Jake walk out to the car with us and at the last minute Jake grabs my arm and pulls his Mets cap down on to my head. I try to take it off but he won't let me, so I get into the car and wave out the back window until we go round a bend and they disappear.

21

We've put it off as long as possible, but it's clear that Gil has to tell Suzanne that Matthew wasn't where we thought he'd be.

Gil stares at my phone, bracing himself, and finally takes out his laptop and writes her an email.

He looks up at me, a little guilty. Do you think I'm a coward?

Only a little, I say, thinking, I wouldn't want to tell Suzanne in person either. I'm guessing that Gil doesn't mention Lynda or Jake in his email; Suzanne is not the sort of woman who would think it was fine to have Matthew's old girlfriend and the son he's never told her about living in his bachelor pad.

I keep wondering how Matthew is going to keep Jake a secret forever. Surely Suzanne will find out someday. If Matthew and Suzanne stay together, how on earth will he explain? There are so many unexploded bombs in Matthew's life. Every day must bring the possibility of discovery. It seems to me like a living hell. Maybe he's used to it. Maybe it's why he left home.

For the first time I'm conscious that Jake is Gabriel's half-brother. Will they meet? Will they grow up to be like their father? Who will I grow up to be like?

I wonder at what point a child becomes a person. Does it happen all at once, or slowly, in stages? Is there an age, a week, a moment, at which all the secrets of the universe are revealed and adulthood descends on a cloud from heaven, altering the brain forever? Will the child-me slink off one day, never to return?

I can't imagine living a real life, or how I'll ever be an adult. It seems like such an unlikely transformation. Someday I may be someone's partner or someone's mother or some-one's forensic pathologist. Someday I may drink too much or have a child I never tell anyone about. Someday I might run away from everything, for reasons of my own.

That me is impossible for present-me to imagine.

I cannot picture me grown up. I cannot picture me any different from the me I am now. I cannot picture me old or married or dead.

Crouching down on the floor with Honey, I press my cheek against her face. She smells warm and woodsy, like dog. Her thoughts are in the moment, not the future or the past. She longs for something she can't define, for a state of equilibrium. If Matthew were to walk through the door now, she would feel complete; her terrible yearning would go. It is impossible to tell her that we may see him soon, or next week, or never. She has only two ways of understanding her situation: *yearning* and *yearning gone*. On–off.

Simple.

I wonder if we should tell Suzanne that we're just filling up time to make ourselves look useful. But that would be like saying *We're really grasping at straws here trying to find some vague connection to the husband who ran out on you and*

Gabriel, leaving no trail at all, because I suppose he doesn't really want to be found. Found by you, anyway. Which feels so close to the truth, barring unexpected murder/suicide/kidnapping, that I really can't bring myself even to think it in the same room as Gil emailing Suzanne, in case she overhears.

I hear the whoosh of the email flying off across New York State and for a moment we both sit perfectly still.

Well? So . . . what next?

Excellent question, Gil says. I guess we return to Suzanne's if we can't think of anything else.

I can't imagine what else we might think of, but I don't say that.

We are failing. Not only that, but we have come all the way from England to fail. When I turn to Gil, he has just closed his laptop and is staring at it, looking as lost as I feel.

Well, Perguntador, he says. We're not terribly good detectives.

But the first rule of being a detective, I tell him, is Do No Harm, and we're not doing any harm, are we?

That's doctors, Mila, not detectives. The first rule of detection is Find Your Man. And we're not doing that either.

A long silence sits in the air and in it we feel separate dejections. Way in the back of my head something nags and nags but I still can't grasp it.

How much do you like Lynda?

Gil frowns. Why on earth do you ask that?

I look at him.

Just the normal amount. It was a long time ago that we were close, he says. What are you thinking? He peers at me closely.

I don't answer.

Then he says, You don't think I'm in love with her? He removes his glasses, rubs his eyes with one hand and replaces them. I'm not. Of course I'm not. He sighs. Perguntador, he says softly. The past is littered with people we've loved, or might have loved. You'll find out in time.

I say nothing for a while. And then, Let's go.

Yes, OK, Gil says, a bit wearily.

I'll bring my charts and maybe we can read something between the lines.

Or allow ideas to connect where they may.

Willy-nilly. At random. I give him a look.

One must have faith.

One does, I say, and take his hand, thinking of all the people he might have loved.

We pack up. I finish before Gil and press my nose to the window. The snow is still falling.

Where does it all come from?

Too many questions, Gil says. Something to do with ice crystals attaching to each other in groups of six. It's pretty odd, when you think about it.

And no two alike.

That's right. Almost makes you believe in God.

Does it make you believe in God?

He shakes his head. No, I said almost. What about you?

No. But no two alike is strange. I wonder how they can be sure.

And who *they* are. Gil is smiling now. The snowflake scientists. Legions of them, catching and examining billions of snowflakes every year, just on the off-chance . . .

And what if they see one they think they recognize but the twin has already melted?

They'd take pictures, wouldn't they? Give them some credit, Mila. They're scientists. They'd be wonderfully scientific.

Does thinking about snowflakes make your head hurt?

Yes, he says.

It make me feel small.

Ah, Gil says. That all depends. If you're right in the foreground, you're huge. In my head, you're bigger than Big Ben or the Andromeda Galaxy. Much bigger.

The Andromeda Galaxy? Really?

Much bigger. Now let's check out and buy some snow gear. This doesn't look like it's going to end any time soon.

Gil pays at reception and they don't charge extra for not checking out at noon.

Doubt we'll be getting much of an influx tonight, the receptionist says. Not many people driving in this weather.

We head back into town. Gil drops me across from the local minimart and drives further up the road to find waterproof jackets and boots for us both, and mittens and matching hats. My job is to stock up on provisions: bananas, apples, bread, jam, sliced ham, cheese. When I've paid for all of that, plus a large bottle of water, there's enough left over to buy a special offer of chocolate marshmallow Wagon Wheels, Rock Bottom Price, Limited Time Only! They're piled high in boxes by the till and, looking at them, I imagine the limited time to be something like forever.

I lug the groceries in the direction Gil headed, and see the car almost immediately. Gil is waiting for me, looking at a map.

I should phone Lynda to say goodbye, he says, and I hand him my phone.

They chat for a few minutes about Matthew, and Gil promises he'll let her know how it all turns out. Goodbye, Lynda, he says at last. Let's not leave it another twenty years. And then he presses end. He looks at what I've bought. Perfect, he says, now let's get going. Apparently there's a storm coming from the east. If we're lucky we'll miss the worst of it.

He hands me back the phone and a few seconds later it bleeps.

Oh god. What if it's Matthew?

But it's not Matthew. It says: **Ta ta old chap. See you in London.**

And it's signed: **Jake**

I wrap my hand over the screen and place it carefully in my pocket.

On the way out of town we stop one last time and I run into the camping supply place where they're advertising cheap blankets on special offer. They're printed like old-fashioned woollen Navajo blankets but made of recycled plastic bottles. The same guy is working and he recognizes me.

Some storm, eh? he says.

We don't have storms like this in London.

London? Is that where you're from?

Yup. London, England.

What're you doing here? he asks, waiting for the receipt to come out of the till.

We're looking for someone who's lost.

His expression tells me that this is a strange and unexpected answer to a polite and ordinary question.

Lost in the snow? His eyes widen.

No. Lost before the snow started. He might not even be lost, for all I know. I guess he knows exactly where he is.

I am aware that he is staring at me.

I sigh. It's complicated, actually.

Yeah, he says, and hands me the bag with the two blankets and the change. I hope you find him.

Thanks.

That is, if you want to find him.

As I get to the door, I turn round and look at him. Yes, I do want to find him. I want to know why he left.

And then I go out.

Well done, Gil says, appraising the bags. I hope we won't need them, but it's better to be safe.

To tell the truth, I don't mind the thought of needing them, imagining Honey and Gil and me curled up like hibernating bears in our car, eating chocolate-covered Wagon Wheels and waiting for the snow to melt.

We set off. It's getting dark. Kids in town are throwing snowballs at each other while their mothers shout at them to stop. The world has turned a deep and dreamy white and I don't ever want to stop looking at it. I think of Jake with a secret thrill that cancels out the sick feeling I get thinking of Matthew.

My eyes shut and the whirling snow takes me into a dream of the cabin and the fire and the music.

We drive for a while, the windscreen wipers skwooshing snow back and forth, the traffic report muttering out of the radio, Gil hunched up over the wheel of the car with his face nearly up against the windscreen, his usual position now. Our headlights light up more snow.

Whenever I open one eye there's nothing but snowflakes. The traffic is moving slowly, and despite worrying that road conditions might make this my last ever journey on earth, I like the feeling of being here in this strange, warm, murmuring place while nature blows billions of non-identical crystals at us.

I glance over at Gil. He hates driving in London, much less in a blizzard in upper New York State with no known destination.

I send another text to Matthew. **If we die in the snow it's your fault.**

And then I text Jake. **See you in London. Xxx Mila**

It's a little risky adding the 'x's when he didn't put any on his, but it might be the last message I ever send so what the hell. Pressing send gives me the feeling that something between us has been sealed.

Gil finds the highway and it's crowded, everyone moving slowly as the snow whirls harder. Occasionally a gust of wind hits the side of the car like a slap and tries to push us out of our lane. Ahead and to the side I see cars skidding. I suppose I should be nervous but I'm feeling strangely flat. There's nothing I can do except not distract Gil. I climb over into the back seat, put my seat belt on and curl up with my head against Honey's back. It's bonier than it looks but she's warm and her breathing is deep and slow. The snowflakes spin and reel and Gil switches over to a classical music station that comes in full of static; I think about Jake, and a cello lulls me to sleep.

When I wake up it's still snowing but we're moving reasonably well. The traffic station is on again – a young woman's voice – and we pass a big snowplough with flashing lights, growling along in the other direction like a great yellow beast.

I lean forward through the gap in the front seats. How far do we have to go?

We'll come off the highway where we can and stay the night, Perguntador. We're not far away. With no weather this would be a breeze.

I wonder what no weather would feel like. White sky, invisible temperature. Comfortable, weightless. I'm not all that anxious to get back to Suzanne's.

The red tail lights ahead all flash on at once and Gil steps on the brake. We slide a little and slow. What's this? he murmurs as we crawl along, until about a mile later the traffic comes to a complete stop. Oh Christ, he says, must be an accident.

And sure enough, after ten minutes sat perfectly still in the snow with the wipers still going and the traffic station blathering about wind and snow like we can't see for ourselves, and the heat blowing out of all the vents, a police car flies past in the breakdown lane followed by another, followed by an ambulance.

There, says Gil. Glad it's not us.

We sit for ages and finally Gil turns off the engine. It's nearly eight, he says, time for supper. So I make us ham and cheese sandwiches with apples and Wagon Wheels for dessert. Instead of dog food, I make Honey a sandwich too. Emergency rations, I tell Gil. Honey takes her sandwich politely and doesn't grab, but then scarfs it down in three bites. She seems restless all of a sudden and I venture out into the snow to walk her. Gil says, Be careful, but nothing's moving. The only danger is losing the car; they all look the same in the snow. But there's a big blue van behind us so we won't get lost. Honey's got an upset stomach and I guess it's the food I've been giving her. She's probably a bit old to change to a whole new diet, even if she likes it better.

We're not out very long but the temperature in the car has dropped. We settle down in the back with my blanket. Gil says he's getting cold too, so I unzip the plastic protector bag and hand him the second one. I can see my breath now but feel cosy enough. We find the local news, in which a government official's arrest for misdeeds gets equal billing with the storm. In London, this would be the biggest news for a century.

I text Jake.

We're stuck on the motorway in the snow. Hope we survive. x Mila

The snow collects on the windows and it's impossible to see out. An hour passes, an hour and a half.

At last Jake texts back. **We call it a highway. Don't freeze to death before I get a chance to visit.**

This makes me smile.

We wait. I doze. Gil listens to the radio.

After what seems a very long time, a policeman with a huge orange jacket looms out of the dark, knocking on the window of every car to make sure we're OK, that we're not elderly and freezing to death, or about to give birth. Sorry, folks, he says, we'll have you moving just as soon as we can. In the meantime, stay warm and don't run your battery down. Well done, he says to us when he sees our blankets. And when Gil answers with a question about the accident, the cop just says, Figures it's a bunch of Brits who come prepared.

His radio crackles and he talks into it. Good, he says. Roger. And signs off.

Dad looks at him enquiringly and he says, We're moving. Got two lanes clear. Start your engine, let it warm up. See you folks later, enjoy your stay in the great state of New York.

I hear him banging on the window of the van behind us.

I wish I could have asked what the accident was, but I didn't dare and he probably wouldn't have told me anyway. I hope it wasn't a whole family killed.

The brake lights of the cars ahead light up and clouds of steam rise from cold engines. I feel a little rush of excitement that we'll be on the move again. A flashing blue strobe light appears inside the car. I look out of the back window and see another police car.

Gil starts the wipers. What a predicament, eh? It's non-stop adventure here in the New World.

There's no arguing with that.

We're moving now, slowly, with a bit of slippage at first but picking up speed, and as we approach the accident, we can see a big grey people mover and a smaller car completely scrunched up beside it. There are a few officials standing huddled around, and some cops directing traffic and shouting at everyone to Keep Moving, Keep Moving! The ambulances have gone.

Gil blinks.

What?

Nothing. I was just thinking about Owen. A highway, a winter's night. Gil shakes his head. Icy roads, maybe.

I close my eyes and imagine how it must have been that night. For the child who died on the road. For the father who survived.

Rubbernecking delays, says Gil. He nods at the cars just ahead of us, passing the accident. *Now* I get it.

Get what?

People craning to see what's happened, in case there's some awful scene of carnage. Rubber. Necks.

I feel ashamed of not wanting to miss it either.

How many years since Owen died?

Gil thinks. Three years, he says, and as he says it, something occurs to him. He must have been just the age you are now.

For some reason this information makes my stomach lurch. I remember the phone call late at night, the news that Matthew's son had died. It didn't mean much to me at the time. People I hardly knew.

Meeting Jake makes Owen seem more real. Also, someone exactly my age being dead makes me think about dying more than someone younger or older. The ghost of Owen will always be the same age as Jake. How could Matthew ever stop thinking about that?

I tap Gil on the shoulder. Why did you and Matthew stop seeing each other?

He glances at me in the mirror, even though it means taking his eyes off the road. We didn't exactly stop seeing each other, he says. When he and Suzanne moved upstate, it just wasn't so easy any more. Not like dropping in when I was in New York City. And I got busy too; I didn't travel to New York so much. Gil frowns. I don't know, sweetheart. Time passes, relationships drift.

And Lynda?

I didn't know anything about that part of his life. It's not the sort of thing Matt would have told me in any case.

Because you fancied her too?

He rolls his eyes. A very long time ago, he says. More likely because it's not the sort of mess you want to talk about.

Even to your oldest friend?

Especially to your oldest friend.

Why not?

People don't like talking about the bits of life that don't add up. The bad stuff. The mistakes.

Do you think he felt guilty?

I don't know. Probably.

Have you done things you can't talk about?

I suppose I have, Gil says. But not lately. And no other children that I know about. You can stop worrying about that at least.

I'm not, I say. But maybe I am. How am I supposed to know what adults are capable of?

Gil doesn't like Suzanne much, which is understandable, because in my opinion, she's not very likeable. But the more I hear about Matthew, the more I think it's not so simple. Maybe Suzanne was fine before she hooked up with him.

We've left the police and the truck and the rubbernecking behind, and are moving at a good pace again. It feels really late, though it's only nine thirty. Look for a place to stop, Gil says.

I need the toilet so we stop at the next service area. The lights seem unnaturally bright after all our time in the car. Gil takes Honey for a walk.

You're right about her stomach, he says. Suzanne will have to wean her off highway food.

For the first time I realize that we'll have to leave Honey alone with Suzanne when we go back to London. If Matthew doesn't show up, that is. What a depressing thought. The nagging feeling has returned but my brain is too tired to think.

It's after ten by the time we find a motel. The car park has been ploughed but the man at the desk apologizes for not having shovelled snow off all the walkways. In the short distance between car and room, we get covered with snow. I use the biggest towel from the bathroom to dry Honey while Gil shuffles back to the car for the rest of our stuff. After a long drink, Honey curls up on her bed in the usual waiting position while Gil props himself up on his bed and pours a large whisky.

The room is warm and although the bedspread is a hideous mix of purple, red and blue, the beds are big and comfortable. After all those hours in the car, it feels luxurious to change into pyjamas and stretch out. Tomorrow we'll be back at Suzanne's and after that, home.

I try Catlin again. **What's happening? How are you? What's the news?** But no answer comes. Gil opens his laptop and I hear the ping of mail. I'm almost asleep; too tired to care who Gil's emailing at this hour.

The last thing I hear is his voice, speaking very quietly into my phone. She's asleep, he's saying, though it won't be true for another thirty seconds or so. See you soon, is the last thing I hear.

See *who* soon? Marieka? Suzanne? At this hour?

The question rumbles through my dreams.

22

In the night I dream about Matthew and Gil. They're the age they are now, but they're acting like kids, sitting up in a tree and throwing stones in a pool of water. In my dream, Matthew loses his balance and slips off the branch and Gil doesn't even reach out to him. He watches his friend fall into the pond, watches the bubbles come up from the place he fell. I stare and stare, more and more panicked, but his head doesn't emerge from the pond, and when I grab Gil's arm and scream that we have to save him, Gil merely frowns and says, There's nothing to worry about, he'll be fine.

But he can't swim! I shout, and Gil answers calmly: It doesn't matter. He can breathe underwater.

I wake up terrified with my heart pounding, relieved to be conscious. Gil has just come in with coffee, a bag of bagels and a carton of orange juice. We're not having Wagon Wheels for breakfast, he says, smiling. Come and have a look outside, it's beautiful.

I had the worst dream, I tell him, trying to shake it out of my head.

Poor you, he says, and sits down on the bed beside me, waiting for me to tell him what it was. But as I go over the dream, the picture that's been trying to take shape in my head for a few days now stutters into focus and all of a sudden I wonder why it's taken so long.

The thing is, Gil doesn't seem all that worried about his friend. Not once on this whole trip has he seemed genuinely anxious or depressed. Not once. Thoughtful, yes. Puzzled, yes. But genuinely, seriously worried? No. And I know him. I know he worries about Marieka when she doesn't phone after a concert or her plane takes off in a storm. He worries about me when I'm late home from school even when I told him in the morning I was staying late or going to someone's house. He doesn't sleep when he's worried and he's slept fine this week. He's even done a bit of work.

Is it that he doesn't care that his friend is drowning? Or perhaps Matthew *can* breathe underwater. Perhaps he's not in danger after all.

I sit very still on the edge of the bed, and luckily Gil is leafing through his papers now, waiting for me to calm down, not noticing.

All of a sudden I'm the one who can't breathe. Gil knows where Matthew is. He knows. I am like Clever Hans. For all my powers of perception I have been unable to add up two and two. I've been so busy reading every other situation around us and drawing flow charts that I didn't pay attention to my own father. It took a message in a dream as clear as a typed letter to tell me that something's going on here that isn't right.

I look at Gil and he looks back at me and his expression flickers. He looks away.

We know each other very well.

So, I say.

So?

So. Let me tell you about my dream.

My father is not remotely as tuned in to the world as I am. But even he can tell that the wind has changed.

OK, he says.

In my dream, I start, you and Matthew are sitting on the branch of a tree, over the swimming pond.

Gil stays very very still.

You're grown-ups, but children at the same time. You know how it is in dreams?

He nods.

And suddenly Matthew falls off the branch, or maybe he jumps in. And I'm there now, and screaming at you, I'm all panicky, shouting, Do something! Do Something! Matthew's drowning! And guess what?

What? says Gil. He looks down.

You do nothing. You tell me he can breathe underwater.

There is a pause. Neither of us says a word.

So, I say. How do you interpret that dream?

Gil still says nothing.

You're not actually worried, are you?

I am, in fact, quite worried, he says.

But not about whether he's dead or not. Not about whether he's killed himself or is missing or anything like that. I glare at him.

He sighs. No.

You know where he is.

My statement hangs in the air.

Yes, says Gil. I do.

You've talked to him?

Email, he says. Mostly.

I cannot *believe* it. Fury overtakes me and, for the first time in my life, I'm actually shouting at my father. I can't *believe* it! What kind of *fake trip* has this been? *It's all just a bunch of lies.*

He rubs his forehead with one hand and reaches out to me with the other but I shove his hand away and move across the bed so he can't touch me.

I'm too angry to speak. Two deep breaths. Four. How long have you known?

Mila, he says. I've been in touch with Matthew since he phoned me in London. He told me he'd left home, but he didn't say why. Or where he'd gone. I said I'd come anyway, as planned, and talk to him when he was ready. He said it was important, that he needed time on his own to think. I don't approve of him leaving home, but he didn't ask my opinion. What else could I do? He pauses and looks at me. He's my best friend.

I'm your *daughter.*

You are. And I'm so sorry I involved you in all of this, really I am, my sweetheart. I didn't know what we were getting into. But, Mila, don't you see? I couldn't tell you I was in touch with him because then you'd have had to lie to Suzanne, and that would have been worse. And in any case, marital problems are . . .

I wait, trembling.

Well. They happen. It's not the end of the world. Especially after all they've been through. He falls silent for a moment. I always regret that I didn't fly over when Owen died. I let

him down. Of course I offered, but . . . it was such a complicated time. And later, when I heard Suzanne was pregnant,
I thought maybe things would be better, that they were
putting their lives back to–

Something occurs to me. *And Marieka?*

He sighs. Mum knows.

I think of the texts she sent me about being good detectives when she knew the whole thing was a fraud. I feel like
smashing something.

So it's a great big *bloody* conspiracy, then. Including everyone but me. Do you actually know where he is?

I didn't until last night, says Gil, very quietly. He emailed
and I phoned him. He wants to see me. At last.

I stare at him, aghast. How can you *ever* expect me to
trust you again?

Very gently, he takes hold of my hands and pulls me
towards him. He looks at me, his eyes hard and soft at the
same time. He takes a deep breath and says, I'm sorry I had
to lie to you. I wouldn't have done it if it hadn't been important. But this isn't about you, my darling.

Why not? I grab my hand back. Why can't it just be a *little
bit* about me and the rest about Matthew? Why does it *all*
have to be about him?

Gil doesn't answer and, for some reason, this makes me
angrier.

What was your plan? To tell me eventually? Or just to
arrive at Matthew's door one day and say, What a coincidence, why, look who's here!

His expression is miserable. I didn't exactly lie to you. I
didn't know where he was. I actually thought he might have

been at the cabin; it seemed worth a shot, anyway. And of course I was going to tell you.

But if you were in touch with Matthew . . . he *knew* we were going to the cabin?

Gil nods.

So you knew he wasn't there?

I didn't know for sure, Gil says, looking away.

But he *knew* what we'd find there?

Gil sighs. I suppose he wanted me to know everything.

He could have sent you a bloody postcard. He's a *control freak*. Joy is right about him. He's a *monster*.

Mila . . . Gil reaches out to me again but I slide away from him. I'm much too upset to acknowledge that there was no way for me to know the truth without being complicit in the lie. I leave the room, slamming the door behind me, and then just walk around in the snow for ten minutes. I make a snowball and eat some of it. The snow tastes wet and concentrated, like chewy water. I hurl the rest of it against the window of our room as hard as I can and it hits with a crash. Fake! I shout, throwing another and another and another. Fake fake fake! But he doesn't appear.

It's cold out here and all I can do is cry. My tears come out hot but are slush by the time they hit my chin.

How did it come to this? This furious me hurling snowballs at a motel window? The me despising my father?

It's freezing cold. I pound on the door and when he opens it, I stand rigid. When he hugs me, I don't hug him back. Tears stream from my eyes.

What is it? I ask, looking up at him at last. Why did he run away? Are he and Suzanne getting divorced?

I don't know, Perguntador. Honestly, I don't. He kisses the top of my head, strokes my hair.

I pull back.

I keep asking myself, Gil says, and I still don't know. It must be a whole combination of things. Us arriving. Guilt over Owen. And Jake. Being a father again. I don't know how I would survive if anything happened to you, Mila. Maybe he doesn't know how to survive either. I guess he'll tell us when we see him.

But what if it's something else? I'm thinking about the gesture Jake made, with the glass.

Something more? Gil frowns. Don't you think enough has happened to him? There doesn't have to be some huge drama, you know. People sometimes just reach a sort of tipping point and . . .

And run away? They *run away*?

I don't know, Mila. I –

But it could be, couldn't it? It could be something else?

I suppose. It could be. He looks at me carefully. What are you thinking?

Jake says he drinks.

When did he say that? Gil appears shocked. What else did he say?

Nothing. He barely even said that. He just did this. I repeat the gesture, a hand tipping, a glass.

Oh my god, Gil says. My god. Could he have been drunk that night? Is that what Jake meant?

I feel like saying, How should I know? Something happened, that's for sure. Something made Matthew unable to face Gil. Something made him leave his wife and baby. I had trouble leaving Gabriel, and I only knew him for ten seconds.

The words Gil said a minute ago hit my brain at last. Did you say *when* we see him? When are we going to see him?

This morning, says Gil.

Oh.

23

When Catlin and I were eleven, we finally did run away from home.

It was Cat's idea but I was happy to go along with it and, as usual, Cat seemed to have sorted all the technical details. How she knew what to do, I had no idea. It was part of her wisdom about the world, like knowing all about sex before anyone else.

The plan was to pretend to head off to school with our rucksacks so as not to draw attention to ourselves, only we'd dump our sports kit and fill our bags with running-away stuff instead.

According to Cat, the biggest danger in running away was starving to death, so we loaded up all the food we could find – biscuits, bread, jam, Cokes, an entire box of After Eights – and set off for the Eurostar terminal. Bring your passport, Cat said, so I did.

When we got to St Pancras we piled our stuff against the wall outside a shop selling watches and jewellery. There were so many students sitting around waiting for trains that no one took any notice of us despite our age. The plan was to say our parents had just gone to buy lunch if anyone challenged us, but nobody did.

Cat told me to guard our things and went off to take a picture of the departures board. Returning, she carefully copied down the train times from her phone into a notebook. Our plan today, she announced, is to get to Brussels, infiltrate the European Parliament, contact our agent there and pass on the computer codes.

Ambitious plan. I wondered who our agent was in Brussels, but knew better than to ask.

Couldn't we just email them? I said. Or send a text?

Cat looked at me like I was insane. Security, she hissed. Everything we do is surveilled to the nth.

I sighed. I didn't think she'd manage to get two unaccompanied eleven-year-olds on a train to Brussels, but you never knew with her. I was fine skiving off school for a day, but unsupervised international travel made me a little nervous.

She stared at her phone and I stared at her, and eventually she looked up and explained that she was waiting for our contact to make himself known. I thought we might have quite a wait ahead of us.

We passed the time practising encryption, which consisted of texting mildly obscene codes to each other. When things got really slow, Cat would send me out to check for enemy agents, or she'd go out to steal chocolates.

By late morning I'd had enough. Can we go home now? I asked Cat.

Soon, she told me. And we went back to code practice, painstakingly translating texts in a bubble of silence surrounded by the boiling chaos of the huge station.

At lunchtime we haunted the cafés set around the long station corridor and got lucky when a pale young foreign couple ordered a lot of food and left most of it behind. We ate the remains of their posh sandwiches and Cat pocketed the tip they'd left, slinking off to check for spies while I faced the waiter's glare.

When it came down to the actual stowing away to Brussels, we pretty much fell at the first hurdle.

Damn them, Catlin growled, patting her pockets furiously, and when I said, Damn who? she said they'd stolen her passport.

It wouldn't have done us any good anyway as we had no tickets and not nearly enough money to buy any, and besides, I happened to know she didn't own a passport so they didn't have to bother stealing it. I know someone who'll forge me a clean one, she said. For a price. And off she shot once more, disappearing into her fantasy.

I sat and watched the crowd, and browsed the bookshop across the way, and eventually returned to our spot and texted **I'm tired** and a few minutes later Cat wandered back and flopped down beside me. About ten minutes after that (which was how long it took to write the average three-word code due to the unnecessary complexity of our cipher) my phone bleeped again and she looked away, as if distracted.

'I love you', said the text. I translated it twice to make sure I'd read it properly and then just sat, not knowing what it meant or how to answer or what to do next.

We stayed like that, a silent island of two, while the crowds flowed over and around us in a steady torrent.

Let's go, Catlin said at last. And without looking at me,

she fastened the flap of her rucksack, stood up, and trudged off towards the Underground station, towing me behind in her wake like an Arctic sledge.

At her house, Cat shot off up the path and I didn't bother to wave. I arrived home at pretty much the exact time I should have been back from school, and went off to my room, where I sat on the bed and thought.

We never were found out. Cat forged sick notes for both of us, knowing I'd forget to forge one for myself, and our teacher accepted them without a murmur. The lack of suspicion was disappointing; Catlin was ready to withstand torture.

I never had the courage to talk to her about the day we almost went to Brussels or to ask about the text. As time passed, I began to think I'd imagined it.

24

I have learned today that my father can lie to me and that I will put all my instincts on hold and believe him because I want to believe that he wouldn't. I didn't discover that he was a murderer or had a secret son, like Matthew. But nonetheless. So much relies on one person assuming the other is telling the truth. If a person can lie to you about one thing, he can lie about something else.

Of course I lied to him too, in a way, but it wasn't the same. Matthew's text was, after all, for me. I was merely protecting Gil from feeling sad. Or was I? Perhaps it was just me thinking I could handle something Gil couldn't.

Another lie.

It makes me think about the nature of truth. I don't lie as a general rule because I've never thought there was much to be gained by it. My parents don't bully me or impose expectations in ways that inspire me to make things up.

I blame the quietness of this arrangement for my innocence. Though it's not as if I've never experienced dishonesty. It starts early in life with girls at school, saying they're only allowed eight friends at a sleepover and you would be the ninth. Or talking about what they've done with some boy when you're pretty sure they haven't. Some lies barely deserve the effort that goes into telling them.

In theory, I would like to lead a transparent life. I would like my life to be as clear as a new pane of glass, without anything shameful and no dark shadows. I would like that. But if I am completely honest, I have to acknowledge secrets too painful even to tell myself. There are things I consider in the deep dark of night; secret terrors. Why are they secrets? I could easily tell either of my parents how I feel, but what would they say? Don't worry, darling, we will do our best never to die? We will never ever leave you, never contract cancer or walk in front of a bus or collapse of old age? We will not leave you alone, not ever, to navigate the world and all of its complexities without us?

They will leave me. It is the first thing you learn that makes you no longer a child. Someday I will die too, but I'm not nearly as frightened of that as I am of being left alone. This is my darkness. Nothing anyone says can console me.

Is Matthew coming here? I ask.

Gil shakes his head. No, we'll go to him. He's staying nearby.

I would hate to have parents who were always looking over my shoulder, reading my diary, checking my thoughts. I would hate to be exposed. And so, perhaps, when I say I long to be a pane of glass, I am lying. I long for partial obscurity at the same time as I long for someone to know me.

25

Matthew is staying thirteen miles from here. His disappearance, when you come right down to it, was modest in scale. For all the driving we've done up and down the state, his big break for freedom took him less than ninety minutes from home.

I am recalculating all the coordinates I've known so far, but am still lost. I take out my phone and text Jake.

We're seeing Matthew today.

I want to tell him more but don't know how. The phone bleeps back almost immediately.

What???

I text back. **Long story.**

There's a pause. I wonder if he's gone and then the phone bleeps again.

Ok. And then a second later: **Report back.**

I will. Wish us luck.

Luck ☺

*

The landscape we drive through is dazzlingly white, every angle and corner softened by great drifts of snow. Icicles have appeared like magic, giant dripping stalactites anchored to the edges of roofs and gutters. I have never held an icicle before and feel an almost unbearable desire to do so. They look precious as fairy jewels and if I broke one off I could wave it about like a sceptre.

I sit in the back with Honey. Gil glances round at us occasionally but says nothing. He holds a map between his knees. I could be helping, but I don't.

We've left the town and are driving through a hilly landscape that's white as far as the eye can see. Fences and stone walls have become soft slopes, and farmhouses wear high slouchy hats. Everything looks clean and new and I like this world of perfection despite knowing that all sorts of barbed wire and dead things lie beneath. The road is clear and black, which makes a change from England, where they'd just wait for it to turn to ice and then melt eventually, while not going to work and complaining that the services can't cope.

I like the way snow piles itself at the top of telephone poles and even collects on the wires in long thin white lines. There are gaps where birds have landed, spelling out Morse-code messages. Dot dot dot. Dash dash dash. Dot dot dot.

We pull off the road into what looks like a low-rent shopping mall and see the MOTEL sign. We're moving slowly now and I'm glad for Suzanne's big car, which feels solid even when we skid.

Gil leaves Honey and me in the car while he goes in. The path is drifted with snow that no one's bothered to re-shovel in the past hour. Gutters all along the front glitter and sag with ice. He comes slithering back out and moves the car nearer to Matthew's part of the motel.

We'll see what happens, he says. As I get out of the car, I step through ice into a deep pool of freezing water. It fills my boot and feels horrible. Honey neatly avoids the puddle. She seems unnaturally alert, head high.

I blame Gil for my frozen leg and follow him up the path, dragging my foot and limping. He ignores me, which is just as well. I'm behaving badly and don't feel like being cajoled.

The girl at the front desk buzzes us in. We follow the corridor round and knock on Matthew's door. I can hear footsteps. Gil looks down at me suddenly and reaches out his hand. I am not so horrible that I refuse to take it. His face is full of anxiety.

I don't recognize the man who opens the door but Honey does. She bounds at him, launching herself through the air like a missile. Darling Honey, I hear him say, laughing, his voice cracked with emotion. Darling dog. Honey is incandescent with joy, ecstatic, and it's contagious. If I had a tail I'd wag it too.

At last.

Matthew buries his head in her thick white ruff. He holds her face in his hands and his tired features fill with light. At last he stands up and embraces my father. Their faces disappear and the two men seem to merge. They could be twins, so similar are they in height and stature. I can imagine them as children, or on the side of a mountain, the closest either had to a brother.

Honey stands looking up at her master, alert to every expression, every inch of her electric with love. She has lost the melancholic expression of the last few days. Matthew cannot resist kneeling again, and she licks his face and neck till he grasps her head in his two hands and pushes her gently away. Not content to step back, she turns sideways and rubs the length of her body across his chest, first one way, then the other. If she could eat him, she would.

Matthew has strong features and unnaturally intense eyes; his hair is thick and grey. Even I can see that despite his age he is handsome. He doesn't attempt hugging or kissing, just looks at me, his head tilted slightly, watching.

It is hard to get over the habit of dislike that has grown in my head, but Matthew is not what I expected. His expression is complex; he looks athletic, but holds his shoulders stiffly, as if in pain. I wish now that I hadn't sent those texts.

While he speaks to Gil I examine his face. There are purple shadows under his eyes. He smells clean and has recently shaved; he wears a faded green flannel shirt. I expected desperation, but instead he is quiet and reserved. It is impossible to ignore the fact that he looks unspeakably sad.

We sit down, me on the bed, Gil and Matthew in chairs. Matthew asks Gil if he wants a drink, doesn't wait for an answer and pours wine into two glasses. I don't need to check my watch. It is not yet ten in the morning. Gil looks ill at ease. When I tune in to my father, the signals all line up. Is this because I know him so well or because he has nothing left to hide?

I get no clear signal from Matthew. What little comes through is scribbly and erratic. Something scrambled is not the same as a lack of information; it suggests interference. Matthew's signals are blocked, as if he has a glass wall buried a few inches beneath his skin. He is accustomed to hiding.

It is fairly obvious that they would like to talk without me present, but I am not in a mood to cooperate. I sit absolutely still, waiting for resolution. Matthew drinks with steady deliberation and pours another. They make small talk about our trip. Gil tells him about Lynda and Jake. Matthew listens quietly, asking questions that may or may not mask a depth of emotional involvement. The mood in the room becomes increasingly odd. Honey searches Matthew's face. I do too, and am abashed, suddenly, to feel that I may be contributing to his unhappiness.

Just as I'm trying to figure out how to excuse myself, Matthew asks if I would mind sitting in the lobby for a bit while they talk. He asks politely, as to a social and intellectual equal. I appreciate this. It is not commonly the way people speak to children. Gil takes me out to the lobby, which has been designed as a pretend study, with a desk, an ugly red leather sofa, a lamp, a small bookshelf filled with paperback books, two chairs and a television. The room is filled with strange light from all the snow outside. No one sits in the reception area, which connects to a small office. Perhaps whoever is on duty hides back there when not required.

Gil kisses the top of my head and apologizes for . . . well, he says, for everything. Then he goes. I look around for Honey and realize that she has stayed with Matthew.

Horrible music is playing through tinny speakers in the

reception area. I get up from the chair and go exploring. All the public areas are empty.

I miss Honey, and despite the fact that she has been Matthew's dog her entire life, I resent her absence. Gil and I brought her here. She should be grateful. Matthew's the one who left her behind with Suzanne. He left Gabriel behind as well. And Jake. But dogs don't hold grudges. At least this one doesn't.

There's nothing else to do but return to the fake study.

I text Jake again. **We found him.**

What do you think?

Not what I expected.

There's a longish pause and I can almost hear Jake thinking on the other end. I wait and wait but no answer comes. Maybe he doesn't know what to say.

I look up and Gil is there, talking in a low voice to the receptionist. She hands him a key.

I've taken a room, Gil says, just for the night. So I can talk to Matt some more.

Matt is nowhere to be seen. We walk out to the car to fetch our bags. I'm waiting to hear what Gil tells me next.

Perguntador.

I'm busy collecting my things and only turn to him after a minute. Yes?

Forgive me, he says. I'm trying to do what's best for everyone.

I stare at him, studying his face. You didn't have to lie to me.

I know, he says.

I'm not an idiot.

Far from it. But everyone alive has secrets, he says. It's terrible being a keeper of them. Worse, maybe, than being kept in the dark.

I say nothing.

Mila, I need your help.

Like he needs to point that out. Our eyes meet again and I feel grubby and false. I am withholding help because it is the only power I have, except the power to be kind.

I reach over and take his hand, the one that is not gripping his suitcase, and so the drama between us melts away.

Who knows? Someday I may need him to lie for me.

26

All pretence of happiness has drained out of our journey. We have settled into our motel room and I feel tired and young. Too young to do what Marieka has asked me to do. Too young to look after my father.

Also, I miss Honey. Why is she so loyal to Matthew but not at all loyal to me?

Gil has come back from another conversation with Matthew. He smells of wine.

What did you find out?

I'm not a very good cross-examiner, he says.

You could just ask him what's going on.

I tried. He doesn't seem to know himself. He says he didn't want me to see him this way.

What way?

Oh, I don't know. Gil shrugs. All of it. It's a mess of a corner he's backed himself into. Whichever way you look at it.

I think about this. And then I think about Catlin.

Maybe he can't bear not turning out better than you.

I can see the cogs in Gil's brain turning. This won't be the sort of thing he'd think of. I wouldn't have thought of it either, without Catlin.

Maybe you remind him of when he was young and hopeful. Before everything went wrong.

It didn't have to be such a mess, Gil says. If it had been just –

But he stops himself. He realizes that saying *just Owen* is impossible. Yet I know what he means. It may be possible to lose a child and survive. But to lose one child and possibly be the reason he's dead? And to have another you've kept secret? And then to leave the third? Even with my incomplete understanding of life I can tell that it's too much. You would begin to twist, like a floorboard cut against the grain. And keep twisting, until it was impossible ever again to be straight.

And *now* to have the friend come to visit. The one whose life you saved. The weaker one.

Gil goes out to find dinner and Marieka picks up on the first ring.

Hello, my dear heart. How are you?

We've found Matthew, I say. Gil was in touch with him all along.

My words hang in the air.

I knew, she says.

Yes.

Oh, my love, she says softly. There is silence on the line and it crackles a little.

I'm fine, I say out loud. But really? I don't feel at all fine.

My sweet girl, she says. Mila, please don't cry. She speaks

so softly now that I can barely hear her. Please, sweetheart. Matthew seemed so . . .

Desperate?

She sounds a bit surprised and says, No, adamant. Do you want to come home?

I want to go home, of course I do. I want to go home more than anything I've ever wanted ever. But I also want to stay with Gil and see this thing through. Maybe now that Matthew is found our job will be over and we can go home together. Maybe now that Matthew is found he will go back to Gabriel and Suzanne and they will all live happily ever after. Maybe it could all still work out.

Marieka's voice interrupts my thoughts. Tell me what you saw, she says. Tell me what you noticed about Matthew.

He looks like Dad.

Yes, Marieka says. Yes, I remember that.

He's very intense.

What else?

But I do not know how to explain what I see – the scribbly signals, the intelligent face, the stiff shoulders, the eerie calm, the dark, dark feeling flowing off him. The wine.

He drinks a lot.

Oh, she says. I wish we hadn't let you go. I should have said no.

We're coming home soon, I say. It's nearly over.

Gil bustles in with bags full of Chinese takeaway so I send Marieka kisses and hand him the phone. They talk softly for a few minutes. I hear Gil say, Yes. No, we haven't talked about it. And then, I know, I know. Soon. I've had enough of this. His voice sounds tired and he rubs his head as if trying to rub thoughts away.

When he hangs up the phone, we talk about Marieka. She sounds worried, he says, and I nod.

She may as well join the club.

Yes, says Gil. She may as well. Let's go home, Perguntador, it's time to go home. We'll leave tomorrow.

But as it happens, we don't.

27

Matthew does not come to breakfast until we are the last people left. He only has coffee and I can see his point. The food is awful, even the toast. Fake jam, fake juice, fake bread. Honey, at least, seems relieved with the outcome of our hunt. She never strays more than a few inches from Matthew's side. When he stands, she stands. When he paces the room, she pads behind him.

Dogs inhabit a world full of different information. Matthew is in the foreground of Honey's life, throwing everything else into shadow, like Big Ben or the Andromeda Galaxy. She fears separation, can smell it hovering around Matthew. If Matthew goes, she will have nothing. Being without him makes her life impossible.

How could he leave her behind?

The receptionist comes in and asks Matthew to move his car to let the snowplough through. I watch from the window as he opens the door for Honey and she jumps in beside him.

Matthew rejoins us, fetching more coffee for himself and Gil. I don't like the look in his eye; it is oddly fixed. He stirs fake milk into the fake coffee but doesn't drink it, instead filling a small glass from a flask he keeps in his pocket. Gil watches, his expression neutral.

The funny thing about Matthew is that he never seems drunk. He seems the same as yesterday. He does not slur his words or fall over or anything.

I take my book and go to another table so they can talk, but it is close enough to hear most of what they say.

Look, Gil says, leaning in towards his friend. It's not too late. You can start again.

Matthew looks up at him. Shakes his head.

You have to want to. Don't you want to?

A loud flat noise makes me jump. Matthew has slammed his hand down on the table. Of course I want to, he says. It's. Too. Late.

There's a long silence and then I hear an awful noise. It's Matthew crying.

There's not another woman? Gil's voice is low.

Matthew actually laughs. No, he says. Not another woman.

Look, says Gil, there's always a way out.

This time Matthew looks up at him, interested, amused. I know, he says.

The two men sit unmoving, each coming to the separate realization that he has misunderstood the other.

The ashes of an old friendship flutter and settle in a delicate heap beneath the breakfast table.

Please, says Gil, and I can hear a rich chattering of emotions in the word. His *please* means *Please* let this all end, *please* let's resolve this so I can go home.

Matthew smiles at him. It'll all be fine, he says.

I want to help.

Oh, I'm well beyond help, Matthew says calmly.

I look over and see Matthew and Gil, their eyes locked across the table, concentrating like chess players.

You're not, Gil says.

No? There is the ghost of a smile on Matthew's face, as if behind the thick dull pain there is a funny side to all of this. I appreciate your faith, he says.

Suddenly I am frightened. My father's faith in Matthew is one of the instruments of his destruction. It reminds him of what he was. How much he has lost.

Matt, come back with us. Come home. Please. Gabriel misses you.

Matthew nods. He looks exhausted.

I'll stay as long as you need me to.

No, says Matthew. Go back to London. There's nothing more you can do.

Are you sure? But I can hear in Gil's voice that he's relieved. No doubt Matthew can hear it too.

Matthew nods. I wonder if he is already drunk, always drunk, in a way that doesn't quite show.

What happened? Ask him what happened that day, Gil, ask him properly, for god's sake. I edge closer, drawn by the dark tug of missing facts.

Gil is still talking, tentatively, saying all the wrong things. I'm sure you can sort things out with Suzanne. For Gabriel's sake.

But Matthew has stopped listening. The very air around him has ceased to move. I look at Gil. Listen! I want to shout. Something happened that day. Something's happening *now*.

176

I am struggling, trying to read a story written in a language I don't quite speak. Why can't Gil translate?

Perhaps Matt chose a brother who would not see into his soul.

The puzzle pieces in my brain dance just out of reach. I turn to Matthew and focus hard.

Gil speaks of getting back to normal. Matthew stares out of fathomless eyes. He sits perfectly still but the hand that grips his glass trembles.

With an air of resignation, Gil gets up from the table and goes to check out, leaving the two of us together.

I focus harder. Gil has told me that in order to translate you need to be a chameleon, to put on the skin of another person, to creep inside his head. I have seen this transformation take place within him – his features and sometimes his personality seem to alter with each voice he takes on, with each book.

And then the pieces begin to line up. I am back on the day of the accident, the day Owen died.

It is dusk.

My head aches, my skin feels tight. Has Matthew been drinking? I can't tell. Owen is sitting in the back seat.

And then I think of Matthew opening the car door for Honey and, *of course*! *Honey* was in the front. Matthew took her everywhere, Suzanne said. She loved the car. So Owen sat in the back because his father's dog was in the front. If their places had been reversed, the child would have lived and the dog died.

With Honey in the front, Matthew had to turn to look at Owen, to talk to him. At that hour, in winter, with ice on the road and everyone driving too fast, that's all it would have taken. One backwards glance. Or two. A lorry coming up from behind.

The picture comes together. *That's* why Suzanne hates Honey. For surviving when Owen didn't. And it's another reason to hate Matthew. For putting Owen in the back. She knew the dog would have been in the front.

Something else occurs to me.

What if Suzanne knew everything? What if she not only knew everything that happened that night, but *everything*? About Lynda and Jake. Matthew's drinking. Maybe she sent him away after Owen died. She'd lost her son and wasn't prepared to lose her husband to a manslaughter charge on the same day. What if she saved him from arrest on the day she was called to the hospital to identify her dead son?

I feel dizzy with the shifting ground of the story. Matthew is staring at me now.

Recalculating, says my brain. Recalculating.

I judged Suzanne to be angry and trivial, the sort of woman who drives people away. But what if she is the hero of the story, the one who has kept all of Matthew's secrets? That's why she never seems to be telling the truth, because it's *his* lies she's hiding. That's why she looks angry all the time.

But now Suzanne has decided that she can no longer lie for him, or has fallen out of love or out of sympathy. Her impulse to protect him has expired. She has fallen in love with someone else.

I meet Matthew's eyes. The contact seems to last forever. It sucks me down into a furious black fog, a muttering hell. I struggle in the cloying dark. Get me out of here, get me out!

And then suddenly everything clears and I tremble with the force of what I see.

Matthew doesn't want some time away, he wants forever. He wants to die. I feel it so strongly it chokes me. He left Honey behind because he didn't plan to come back.

His eyes are intense and serious. He seems surprised and – could it be? – slightly amused by what has passed between us.

I am floating up to the ceiling, looking down on this scene. I can't speak.

Gil returns with the room key and a printout of our bill. His smile fades when he sees us and he looks from one to the other, puzzled. But Matt is a conjurer of moods and he sets questions for Gil to ease the moment: When will you return to London? How is Marieka? Will you see Suzanne?

I turn to leave and my chair slides back more violently than I intend, tipping backwards with a crash.

Honey leaps to her feet, her whole body poised, a low noise in her chest. I wonder how far she will go to protect him. Would she tear out my throat?

Come on, Gil says to me, let's pack up. I've got some calls to make, he says to Matthew, who nods assent. We'll leave in an hour. You can follow us when you're ready.

I text Jake. **It's awful here.**

And within seconds he texts back. **It'll be over soon.**

Which is true, one way or another.

28

Gil phones Suzanne and talks for a long time. I am glad not to be included. I want to go back to being a child.

There are hundreds of channels on American TV and I flick through without paying much attention to anything on the screen. It is mostly commercials. I come to the high numbers, where a topless woman rubs her breasts and starts to ask if I want to get to know her better before I click past. I pause on a nature show where a quiet-voiced man admires a beautiful stag in a clearing, saying, Isn't he a magnificent creature? and then raises his rifle and shoots him through the heart. The animal staggers and falls to his knees. I want to throw up.

A week ago America felt like the friendliest place in the world but I am starting to see darkness everywhere I look. The worst thing is, I don't think it is America. I think it is me.

Gil phones Marieka next. I don't hear much of what he's saying. It's OK, he says. We'll be there before you know it.

He's too worried to lie to anyone now. He's worried for Matthew, as well he should be – the time I spent in Matthew's head felt like drowning. Maybe he's even worried for me.

I slip under Gil's arm so that he has to hold me close. I wish he could clasp me tight enough to squeeze the images out of my head. They are not real pictures but they are more vivid than any I have ever seen. I do not need to close my eyes to see them.

Gil, I say. Do you think Matthew will be OK? What if he does something desperate? I look intently at my father. Think, I beg him silently. Look at your friend. Figure it out.

Gil tightens his arm round me. Don't worry, Mila. Matthew will sort himself out. He always does.

I want to tell my father that maybe this time he won't sort himself out. But I am twelve years old, should I be the one to know?

Make him promise to come home with us, I beg. *Please.* Gil looks surprised. Make him *promise.*

OK. I'll make him promise.

Just then my phone rings and Gil reaches over to answer it, fumbling the buttons but eventually hitting the right one. He says hello and then, to my surprise, hands it over.

CAT!!

Dad's moved to Leeds, she says, with no preamble, not even hello.

No! I say. *Leeds?*

With his girlfriend.

His *what?* Are you kidding?

Ha ha ha, she says grimly. Yes, I are making the funny joke.

That's awful! Have you met her?

Despite the distance between us, I can see the expression on her face. Yeah, she says. I've met her.

I don't suppose she's nice?

Evil viper troll-bitch from hell.

Oh, Cat. I'm so sorry.

I don't care if I never see him again. Mum hates him too. She says she's damned if she'll pay for me to visit him. Are you still there?

Yes, I'm here. I'm coming home soon. We'll make voodoo dolls.

Perfect, she says. How's my egg?

Oh Christ, her egg. It's big all right, I say. How's mine?

I've been far too busy having my *life wrecked* to think about chocolate, she says, in her most self-righteous voice.

Neither of us says anything.

Are you having fun in America? Her voice is sulky.

Fun? I say. For some reason this strikes me as hilarious. Fun? I say again, and start to laugh. Not really, Cat. Not really very much actual so-called *fun*. What I'm having is what you might call the *opposite* of fun. *Anti-fun*.

Perfect, says Cat, and that's it, I'm off, laughing so hard I can't stop.

What do you mean *perfect*? I can barely choke out the words. What kind of friend are you?

The best kind, she says, trying to sound serious but giving way to snorts of hilarity. It would be *unbearable* if you were having the time of your life while I suffered the torments of hell. At the words *torments of hell* she explodes into guffaws, which sets me off even more.

Tears are running down my face and I'm about to answer that the torments of *her* hell are nothing compared to the torments of *mine*, but there's a click and she's gone.

Gil comes back into the room and looks at me quizzically but I just groan and dry my eyes on my sleeve.

My sides actually ache from laughing so hard and for a minute I can't move.

I love you too, Cat, I want to say, even though the phone line is completely silent and my answer is a year too late.

29

We drive back to Suzanne's in silence. Neither of us is looking forward to this reunion.

I don't know what Gil said to him, but Matthew arrives an hour after we do and Suzanne walks out to the car to greet him. They embrace and she drops her head on to his shoulder. For an instant the flow of emotion between them is powerful, unmistakeable. But she pulls away too soon, her lips pursed tight. His eyes search her face but she turns away.

Gabriel flaps his hands up and down like a penguin when he sees me. He starts to laugh and say me-me-me, which could be his version of Mila. I scoop him up, kiss him noisily on his fat neck to make him laugh even more and bounce him up and down. Gabriel B-B-B-Billington! Silly Billy Billing-ton!

But when Matthew appears, Gabriel's happiness hits a different note. He would fly out of my arms if only it were possible.

Matthew catches him up and the two spin round, gabbling in some private language. Honey watches quietly. When at last they stop, Gabriel reaches over a bit dizzily and grabs my hair with one fist. He holds on to steady the world, then shifts, his face suddenly serious, closes his eyes and lays his head against Matthew's chest. He is a simple mechanism, like a toy aeroplane with a twisted-up rubber band to make him fly. When the rubber band untwists, he falls to earth. I remove his hand from my hair, opening each finger softly, but grateful, somehow, for the gesture. He is nearly asleep.

Suzanne comes out of the kitchen and takes him off Matthew, saying it's time for bed and that she's made sandwiches for us if we're hungry. She disappears with Gabriel and we can hear the bath running.

I look at the sandwiches Suzanne has made – cheese and tomato on brown bread – and am suddenly ravenous. We sit on high stools at what she calls the breakfast bar and eat our supper. Gil opens a beer and holds it out to Matthew, who doesn't take it.

None of us speaks. After a minute or two, Matthew gets up and leaves the room. We hear his tread on the stair. A door closing.

What did we expect to find when we set out? Something nice? Did we imagine Matthew ran away to join the circus? That it was like searching for a lost cat, one you might find up a tree, grateful to be rescued? Frightened cats will claw you to pieces when you try to save them. I glance at Gil. Did he not think any of this through?

A gulf has opened between us and I am angry. I am a child, I want to shout at him. *Protect me.*

My head hurts. Despite a greater than average ability to see clearly, I have been conned. The people I have expected to take care of me – the wise ones, with life experience – have got it wrong.

I return to my room (Owen's room), climb under the covers fully clothed and pull the dark woollen blankets up over my knees and head, like a tent. It's boring being with messed-up people all the time and after all those hours and days in cars and motel rooms I have a desperate urge to be by myself, to escape the tension in the house and the failure of our trip. (Was it a failure? Or an unhappy success?)

The snow is nearly gone but a wild wind whips the trees against my window. Under the pillow is Suzanne's (Matthew's?) book on caravanserais; I slip it out and illuminate the camel's strange head on the cover with my phone torch. Long red and gold tassels decorate his bridle, which is set with discs of hammered silver. A low building with a teardrop-shaped entrance covers the background. I turn the pages past beautiful photographs of tents and woven rugs and men with burning eyes and imagine other journeys, with camels instead of cars and palm dates instead of sandwiches; messengers moving in long slow arcs across empty deserts with news of life and death.

Caravanserai.

I close my eyes and imagine the cool interior of the rest stop, the whitening sun. After the endless bounce and sway of the camels, the ground feels unsteady. They drink, noses deep in stone troughs. Twenty gallons. Forty. Fifty.

If I were on the Silk Trail I could cross Persia, China, Arabia. Just for a while, I would be happy moving through empty spaces, knowing no one, living a different life.

I close my eyes and think about Jake.

30

Matthew and Suzanne speak politely, their faces empty of feeling.

She has moved out of the house, returning with Gabriel so he can see Matthew, who only comes alive when they are together. I am touched by father and son; you don't have to be a genius to recognize that they are full of love for each other. Honey lies beside them, forming a holy trinity. She does not take her eyes off Matthew, and he, in turn, keeps one hand laid gently on her head or back nearly all of the time. Suzanne is staying, she tells us, with a friend. I think it is probably more than a friend but I'm tired of knowing things.

Down the phone line I hear Marieka's sharp intake of breath. What sort of friend is she staying with? Who is it?

But this I can't answer. Age, height, colour of eyes? I am not the KGB.

I have barely spoken to Matthew since we returned.

Our last day is sunny and Matthew and Gil work outdoors to keep busy. They dig up the garden, each working a different end, absorbed in different thoughts. Or the same ones, thought separately. Honey lies nearby with her head on her paws, constantly alert. I cannot bring myself to be inside her head.

Our flight is tomorrow. Easter Sunday.

I sit with Gabriel and draw eggs for him in bright crayons and he slaps them triumphantly with his hands and shouts Ek! I get overconfident and try ducks and bunnies, but they don't look right. He recognizes them though, despite my wobbly pictures, and I wonder how he translates bad drawings of ducks and bunnies into the animals he sees at the zoo or the park. Three dimensions into two, feathers and fur into pink and yellow crayon. An ordinary miracle.

Duck! he says proudly and points. And then, Ek! Has he ever seen a painted egg? Or only the ones his nanny scrambles sometimes for his breakfast? She uses brown ones that look nothing like the ones I've drawn. How can he decode the world so expertly?

We are all together for one last night, Gabriel in his pyjamas with feet, Suzanne making dinner as if this were still her home. But no one is fooled. She is like a horse whose eyes have turned to the next jump.

Matthew pours wine for his wife and his friend but not for himself. The conversation is stilted and he and Suzanne never address each other directly. When I offer to set the table, she looks grateful and then, instead of simply handing me the cutlery, she places it carefully in my outstretched hands and closes her fingers round mine. I look up into her eyes.

I'm sorry, she says in a soft voice meant only for me. I'm sorry we made such a mess of your holiday . . . and everything else. She shrugs and clasps my hands tighter for an instant before releasing them. It's all a mess, she says. A big fucking horrible bloody mess.

Her eyes swim with tears.

It's OK, I tell her. It's not your fault.

No? she says, pushing the hair off her face and almost smiling. I don't know any more. Maybe it is my fault. She turns away.

I set the table and Suzanne calls everyone in to dinner. We make small talk that no one will ever remember and directly after dinner, Suzanne fetches Garbriel and kisses Gil and me goodnight.

As she turns to leave, Matthew stops her and takes Gabriel from her arms. The child is more asleep than awake, but he wraps his arms tightly round his father's neck and Matthew kisses his cheek, pressing his face against Gabriel's, before gently freeing the child's arms and giving him up to an impatient Suzanne.

Gil follows her out to the car, leaving me with Matthew, and I'm desperate to escape, panicked at the thought of another confrontation. But before I can follow Gil, Matthew stops me.

Don't worry, Mila, he says. It'll be OK.

I shake my head. No it won't.

He tilts his head slightly, enquiringly.

What sort of person are you? Anger chokes me. Have you even thought about how Gabriel will feel? Or Honey? It's not just you. It's not just your life.

I know that, he says.

Well, if you know then how can you consider *doing it*? I cannot bring myself to say the words: *killing yourself.*

It's complicated, he says. You'll understand someday.

I understand *now*, I shout at him. I understand that your life is a mess. But I don't understand how you think *that* is going to make it better for anyone but you.

You're not an ordinary child, Matthew says.

What about what you told Gil? I say, ignoring him. About not lying down in the snow? Gil always remembered. You're the one who's forgotten.

I haven't forgotten, Matt says.

Then *don't do it*.

We stand facing each other, squared off. I'm breathing hard. One minute Matthew is there; the next he has turned inward, as if I am no longer in the room.

I follow Gil out to the car.

Suzanne arranges Gabriel in his car seat and clicks the seat belt, which swings over his head in one piece like the roof of a fighter jet. She circles round to the driver's side of the little blue car (whose?) and then she and Gil talk about the airport and the times of our flights. I lean in to kiss Gabriel's fat cheek in the dark, tears dripping from my face on to his. He is fast asleep, his hands grabbed into fists, his eyes screwed up as if battling an unseen foe. He opens his eyes for an instant and blinks and smiles, but he's not properly awake and a second later he's out once more. I kiss his damp fist and hope his sleep is not always full of shadows, then shut the car door as quietly as I can.

Over at the front door of the house, Honey and Matthew stand looking out at us, framed in a halo of light, suspended between this world and the next.

31

The following morning, Matthew and Gil take our bags out to the driveway to wait for Suzanne. The two men embrace. There are no speeches, no final words.

Matthew stands back a little and looks at me carefully.

Take care of Honey, I say to him, and he nods. And Gabriel.

He nods again.

And you, I say.

And you too, Mila, he says.

He disappears into the house before Suzanne arrives, alone. Gabriel is at playgroup, she tells us. We pile our bags into her car and set off. No one speaks. At international departures in New York, it is impossible to stop for more than a minute or two, so our parting is brief. A quick hug and Suzanne is gone.

As we check for passports and arrange ourselves at the terminal, Gil hands me an extra bag to carry, a large one with handles.

I peer inside and there it is – the cowboy Easter egg, vast and unwieldy, the box a bit shopworn. I look up, astonished.

He took some convincing, Gil says. Oh yes. Hi ho, Silver. It took some doing, all right.

I'm gaping at him. What on earth did you say?

Gil shakes his head. Shouldn't tell you, really. I told him I worked for Frommer's. Updating travel guides for the European market.

You didn't.

Gil nods. I did. It was amazing. He practically forced the thing on me. Wouldn't take a penny.

At this moment, I am loving my father almost to distraction. You're a genius, I say, grinning. I'm so proud. Cat will love it.

But secretly it's I who loves it, loves Gil for going back with his extremely clever, extremely dodgy story. His lie, actually.

How on earth will it go on the plane? I ask him. You could fit a family of four in that egg. We'll be arrested for smuggling.

It's your problem now, Gil says. I've done my bit. He picks up the rest of the bags and heads off.

I refuse to check the egg with my luggage, so they attach a tag and a big red sticker reading FRAGILE, and I lug it through departures and on to the plane and manage to wedge it up in the overhead locker. It takes up nearly the whole space.

I should have bought it a seat, Gil says.

We stow our bags and do up our seat belts and the captain says there'll be a half-hour delay before take-off. Gil opens his book and is gone from me. I don't bug him, knowing he will remain silent until he has thought everything through. It might be a few minutes or a few hours or a few days.

I'm leafing through the in-flight magazine when my phone bleeps. I hope it's Jake, but when I open the message, it says:

Goodbye Mila

I'm glad Gil isn't paying attention.

Goodbye Matthew I text back, wishing there were something I could add, something old-fashioned like *fare thee well* or *godspeed*. And then, on impulse, I paste Jake's contact details into the text. And press send.

Outside of my window the planes turn, speed along the runway, rise up and are gone. Gradually, as we wait to take off, I begin to shed some of the sorrows of this journey. Watching planes take off makes me feel like a child again, like Gabriel shouting *Again, again!* We're something like twenty-eighth in line; the repetitive magic soothes me.

At long last our plane turns on to the runway, the engines roar and I'm about to turn off the phone when it bleeps one last time.

See you soon it says. And is signed **Jake xoxo**

I quickly switch it off and snuggle down in the seat. For the moment, all I care about is this.

So much of translating, Gil once told me, takes place in an imaginary space where the writer and the translator come together. It is not necessary to sympathize with the writer, to agree with what he's written. But it is necessary to walk alongside and stay in step. It's harder, he says, when the other person has a bad limp or stops and starts all the time or moves erratically. It is hardest of all when the story comes from a place the translator himself can't go.

193

We have been in the air for two hours when he turns to me. Very gently, he takes hold of my hands in both of his.

What a thing to have put you through, he says, shaking his head. I'm so sorry. I should never have brought you here. I thought . . . I don't know what I thought. I thought that it was just a blip, that everything would be OK.

Maybe it will be.

He nods. It's up to Matthew.

I look at him. Do you think he was drunk the night Owen died?

Gil shrugs. Does it matter? The child is dead and everything else that follows has followed.

For a while we say nothing.

Well, I say at last. At least he has Honey.

Yes . . . Gil draws out the single syllable and looks at me. But Honey's a dog.

He says this as if it's something I've failed to notice, but I can see what he's thinking: a dog isn't the most important thing.

And I think, OK. So a dog isn't the most important thing. But a dog like Honey loves one person completely, unwaveringly, with perfect faith. That has to be more important than most things.

And Gabriel, I say. He has Gabriel too.

Gil says nothing but I know the answer. The answer is that Gabriel can't save Matthew any more than Gil can, or Honey. Or Jake. But we are all woven together, like a piece of cloth, and we all support each other, for better or worse. Gabriel is just a baby but eventually he will see the world and his father as they are: imperfect, dangerous, peppered with betrayals and also with love.

I cannot think about these things any longer. I droop against Gil and inhale the familiar scent of him, and he puts his arm round my shoulders and tells me to go to sleep now, not to worry about anything.

The world will trundle along, he says, and kisses the top of my head. Despite us thinking it must grind to a halt. The world has seen worse than us, Perguntador. It is not so easily shocked.

I rest against him, aware of how tightly we are bound together, through thick and thin. For the moment I have stopped thinking of a time when we will no longer have each other. Marieka was right to tell me to take care of Gil. He and I will watch over one another for as long as we are alive, and Marieka will watch over us both, each of us according to our capacity for care. I will not always be happy, but perhaps, if I'm lucky, I will be spared the agony of adding pain to the world.

And then I close my eyes and drift off to the great white noise of the engines, dreaming of a future I know nothing about.

how
I live
now

winner of the
Guardian Fiction Prize

DON'T MISS THE MAJOR FILM
meg rosoff

'Intense and startling . . . heartbreakingly romantic'
– *The Times*

WINNER OF THE CARNEGIE MEDAL

The author of the brilliant *How I Live Now*

meg rosoff

'Intelligent, ironic and darkly funny'
– *Time Out*

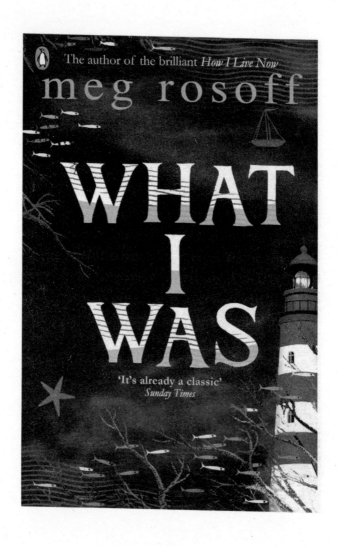

The author of the brilliant *How I Live Now*

meg rosoff

WHAT I WAS

'It's already a classic'
Sunday Times

'Thrilling and sensitively told'
– *Observer*

'A wonderful, captivating writer. 5 *****'
Daily Telegraph

THE
B RIDE'S
FAREWELL

The author of the brilliant *How I Live Now*

meg rosoff

'Rosoff's writing is luminously beautiful'
– *Financial Times*

'Genius'
ANTHONY HOROWITZ

WHAT IF GOD WERE
A TEENAGE BOY?

THERE
IS NO
DOG

The author of the brilliant *How I Live Now*

meg rosoff

'A wild, wise, cartwheeling explanation of life,
the universe and everything' – Mal Peet